SEVEN SLEEPERS **THE LOST CHRONICLES** 7

The
Terrible
Beast
of ZOR

GILBERT MORRIS

MOODY PRESS
CHICAGO

ISBN: 0-8024-3673-0

1 3 5 7 9 10 8 6 4 2

Printed in the United States of America

Contents

1
The Dark Hour

The Royal Council of Madria was gathered around the long table, a table that occupied most of the room. They waited quietly, and Dethenor, Head of the Royal Council, was the quietest of all.

Dethenor was a thin man with long silver hair and gray eyes. The only sign of his high office was the round golden medallion that dangled from a gold chain about his neck. He fingered the medallion now as he glanced around the table, fixing his eyes briefly on each face.

All of the Council members were men of age and experience, and Dethenor trusted most of them. But things were going badly in Madria, and a trace of apprehension shot through him even now as he considered the perils that lay before the kingdom.

At the other end of the table sat Count Ferrod, nephew of King Alquin. Ferrod was a short man, heavy, with close-set brown eyes and thinning brown hair. Dethenor noticed that Count Ferrod's gaze too was moving from face to face, and Dethenor knew very well what was happening.

He's thinking of how to influence the Council again. And I must not let him do it. Once again he found himself thinking, *After Prince Alexander, Ferrod is next in line for the throne—and little could be worse than to have him become king of our land!*

The doors at the far end of the council room swung open, and two guards clad in green uniforms trimmed in gold held them back. The first to enter was

Alcindor, the young military aide and right-hand man to the king. Alcindor was almost like a son to the king —*perhaps even more of a son than Prince Alexander himself,* Dethenor thought.

Alcindor's eyes swept the room quickly, and his hand rested on the sword hilt at his side. He was always careful with the king's life, even in the apparent safety of the council room. Dethenor knew a moment of relief, because here was one loyal subject at least.

All stood, and every eye turned to the man who entered now. King Alquin had always been a strong, healthy, athletic man, skilled in all the arts of war. Now, however, the muscles of his body were shrunken, and he was bent over in an unnatural slump. His hair was gray, and lines were etched across his face. He painfully crossed the stone floor to the table only with the help of his wife.

Queen Lenore, in contrast, was a beautiful woman, tall and statuesque and strong. She too was older, but her auburn hair was still free from gray, and her eyes were bright and watchful as she too surveyed the Council.

She helped the king make his way to the heavily carved oak chair at the head of the table, and Dethenor, who would sit next to him, said quietly, "Welcome to the Council, Your Majesty."

King Alquin sat down, holding onto the massive arms of the chair. He moved slowly and carefully as a man who had been terribly wounded and had learned to adapt himself to the pain. He nodded to Dethenor, saying in a strained voice, "I am glad to see you, Chancellor."

Queen Lenore took a seat on the opposite side of the king, and the aide moved to his accustomed position immediately behind him. The young man's eyes still moved restlessly, and not for one moment did he relax his vigilance.

King Alquin drew himself up in the chair, and his gaze traveled from face to face. The king knew these men well, Dethenor thought. He himself had chosen all of them for his counselors. There was only one empty chair at the table, and pain came to Alquin's expression when he looked at it.

Dethenor knew instantly what was occurring in his mind. *He's grieving that Prince Alexander is not here*, Dethenor thought, *and so am I. It's the prince's place, and again he has not seen fit to attend.*

"I think we will dispense with the ordinary business today," King Alquin said in a shaky voice. He shifted uncomfortably, and Queen Lenore leaned forward and put a hand on his arm. He gave her a brief smile, then his face turned very solemn. "What is the word from Zor?"

"It is not good, I'm afraid, Your Majesty," Ferrod answered. The count's eyelids drooped, giving him almost a sleepy expression. His garment was encrusted with jewels and gold, and he wore a magnificent stone on the middle finger of his right hand.

"The news from Zor is never good," King Alquin said wearily. "Then, what is the word from my army?"

"I have just received a message from Captain Asimov."

Dethenor watched Ferrod take a sheaf of parchment from his inner pocket.

The count began to read it aloud.

"The armies of Zor are pressing us heavily at every position. We must have reinforcements at once, or all will be lost. Numbers of our men have been killed or wounded, and a detailed report follows. I recommend that we pull back and give up our present position."

Alcindor snorted. "He always recommends that we pull back!"

"He is the captain of our army!" Count Ferrod said angrily. "We must trust his expertise!"

"I agree with Alcindor."

Dethenor—indeed everyone—looked at the queen. Queen Lenore seldom spoke in council. But she spoke now, quietly. Her voice was clear and steady, though quite low. "We must hold the lines where they are. Once we begin to retreat—there is only one end to that."

"But, Queen Lenore, we *cannot* hold the lines!" Ferrod protested. "Every day we are losing men, while the enemy grows stronger."

The debate went on for some time. The king listened for a while, saying nothing. Finally he looked over at the chancellor. "Lord Dethenor, what say you?"

"I agree with the queen." He fixed his gaze on Count Ferrod and waited for him to object, but the count was silent. "We must hold our lines. We must protect our kingdom!" He looked up at the aide. "Alcindor, what would you advise?"

Alcindor had grown up as a soldier. Though he was young, he and the king had been in many battles together, and now that the king was too feeble to go out to fight, he still knew the king's heart. Dethenor was sure of that.

Alcindor stepped over to a map that was pinned to the wall and said, "Here is our kingdom of Madria." His fingers swept in a circle. "Here are the Madrian Mountains that encircle us. They are a natural protection. As long as we hold the mountain passes, we can keep the Zorians out. But once they break through, there is nothing to stop them from sweeping in on us. I say we send every available man and hold the mountain passes at all cost."

Ferrod shouted, "It's impossible! We only have a limited number of men. We are already heavily out-numbered."

Dethenor listened for a time as Ferrod argued on. Finally he glanced at the king and interrupted. "Enough, Count! So what do you say, Your Majesty? What are your commands?"

King Alquin replied immediately, "Alcindor is cor-rect. We must hold the mountain passes."

"But, Your Majesty," Count Ferrod protested, "be reasonable. Valor is one thing, but throwing away our lives for nothing—that is something else."

"Would you have us to just give up our country?" the king demanded. His eyes flashed, and he sat up straighter in the carved oak chair. There was a hint of kingliness and power in him still as he said, "We will *never* surrender to Zor!"

"It's not a matter of surrender, sire," Count Ferrod kept on. Now he lowered his voice like a conspirator and leaned forward. "All that the Zorians ask is that we pay tribute to them once a year."

"And we all know where that will end," Dethenor said grimly. "The Zorians are not to be trusted. If we give them one inch, they'll take another—and then another—until finally they will rule over us entirely."

"You are correct, Dethenor. They would make slaves of us," the king said. "Send orders to Captain Asimov to hold the lines. We will send him what reinforcements we can. This Council is dismissed."

All except the king, the queen, Alcindor, and Dethenor rose and left the council chamber.

Dethenor waited until the door was closed. Then he said, "Your Majesty, I must say it again. Prince Alexander must cease his ways and join us. The people must have a prince to look to in times such as these."

"I know. I know. You are right, Dethenor. I am too frail to go out and fight, and the people need to see a prince fighting for them. Otherwise *they* will not fight."

The room grew quiet, as everyone was probably thinking the same thing.

Finally Alcindor spoke his thoughts aloud. "The prince must be urged to assume his rightful role, Your Majesty. There is no other way."

"Alcindor is right," Dethenor agreed quickly.

The king looked at his wife, and a silent message seemed to pass between them. "We have spoiled him, Lenore," he said quietly. "We gave him everything—and now he has become a wastrel."

"Perhaps it is not too late, my husband," Queen Lenore said. "I know he has taken a wrong path, but there is good in him. He is of your bloodline. We must do whatever is necessary to bring him to what he should be."

King Alquin's gaze met that of Alcindor then. "Go," he said. "Summon the prince."

"What if he refuses to come?"

"Bring him here in chains if you must!" And a steely note had crept into the king's voice.

Alcindor's eyes glinted. "Yes, sire. It shall be as you say."

Grenda, Ferrod's wife, was waiting at the council chamber door. They spoke in whispers as they started down the hall.

Briefly he told her what had happened. "He is set on continuing the war."

"Foolishness! Insanity!" Grenda spat. She was an attractive woman with black hair and black eyes, but the eyes were angry. Abruptly, she murmured, "You are the next in line for the throne."

"Be quiet, Grenda! It is treason to even speak aloud of that."

"It is only wisdom. The king may die soon. Indeed, everyone thinks he will. His wounds will not heal. That leaves only Prince Alexander, and he is a worthless young scoundrel."

"He is still the prince."

Grenda's eyes glittered. "Many things may happen to a young man—sickness, accidents. Perhaps he will even go to fight in the war. If he dies, and Alquin is gone, you will be the king."

Ferrod hesitated. Then he nodded. "And you," he said, "will be the queen." He saw the approval in her eyes.

2

The Dark Stranger

The small ballroom was packed to capacity. In one corner a group of four musicians plied their instruments, spilling music into the room. The friends of Prince Alexander were gathered to find whatever pleasure was available.

"Prince Alex, drink up!"

The speaker was a beautiful girl. She carried a tray of golden goblets filled with wine and held it out to the prince.

Young Prince Alex took a cup, then said, "You always bring me luck, Sophie. Stand by me while I win the money of all these so-called gamblers."

The prince was seated at a table with four men. As they continued to play, the gold began to flow from the prince to those who sat around him.

"Your good luck is bad today, Prince Alex," one of the players said. He was a small man with bright brown eyes and pale skin. Like the others, he was richly dressed. He wagged his head in mock sadness. "If you were not the prince, you would have been bankrupt long before now."

"Vain, that's one of the advantages of being a prince."

Laughter went up around the table.

The man Vain had just said, "I propose a toast," when the door swung open, and everyone turned to look. The prince—and probably all the others—expected to see another of his friends.

The newcomer was Alcindor.

Vain suddenly grew very watchful. "Hello, Alcindor," he said loudly. "Don't tell me you've come to join our party."

Alcindor was wearing the green-and-gold uniform of the royal guard. His sword was at his side, and a leather strap crossed his breast.

"No, I have not come to join your gambling party, Vain. I am here on assignment from the king."

The room fell silent, and Alexander thought Vain's face paled a little.

Vain started to speak, but the prince interrupted him.

"Oh, sit down, Alcindor!" he said. "You never have any fun! Don't you have anything to do but play soldier?"

Alcindor's eyes swept the room in a look of disgust.

The prince well knew that his father's aide had never had any patience with Alexander's friends. He always claimed they followed after the prince for what they could get out of him. But Alex did not believe that.

Alcindor ignored the others and spoke directly to the prince. "You are summoned to appear before the king, Prince Alexander."

Alexander blinked rather stupidly. It took a moment for the meaning of the tall soldier's words to become clear. He glanced across the table at Vain, who winked at him and said, "My, it sounds as if you're going to get a spanking from your papa."

"Enough of that, Vain!" Alcindor said almost fiercely.

"Now you wait a minute!" the prince said. "Don't talk to my friends that way, Alcindor."

"I didn't come to talk to your friends. I came to escort you to the king."

Alexander was aware that everyone was watching. They had teased him before about being brought to heel by his parents, and he felt his face flush.

"I'll be along after a time, Alcindor," he muttered. He turned back to the table. "Now, let's play cards."

Alcindor's voice cut through the room like a sharp knife. "The king commands me to bring you now, Prince!"

"I said I would come later! Now, get out of here!"

Alcindor's lips grew tight, and his eyes glinted. "My prince, you force me to do this. You will either come peaceably, or I will take you forcibly."

"You cannot force me to do anything!"

"I am the servant of King Alquin, the monarch of this kingdom," Alcindor said. He stepped forward and towered over Alexander. "His orders are to bring you at once! And, specifically, if you will not come of your own will, I am to bring you under guard."

Alexander pushed back his chair and stood up. He glared at the aide. "You wouldn't dare touch me!"

Alcindor took another step forward and gripped his arm. "I'm sorry that you will have it no other way, but you are going to see the king. Now."

Vain suddenly lunged out of his chair. "Turn him loose!" he shouted. "This is treason!"

Alcindor's fist moved swiftly, and the prince saw Vain fly backward. He crashed into a table loaded with silver trays and dishes and cups of wine, and a tremendous clatter followed.

"Do any of the rest of you care to protest?" Alcindor asked quietly. He looked about almost hopefully, but the sudden and absolute devastation of Vain apparently stopped them. Nobody moved to help the fallen man, who was lying as still as if he had been struck with a mace.

"I didn't think so," Alcindor said. "Come, Prince Alexander. The king awaits you."

"Wait a minute—"

But Alexander had no choice. The powerful hold on his arm was enough, and he felt himself dragged from the room, stumbling and almost losing his balance.

"Take the prince's arms and follow me!" Alcindor ordered the two soldiers who waited at the door. The command was curt. "If he falls, pick him up and carry him!"

The soldiers' strong grip dragged Prince Alexander against his will out of the tavern and into the street. He was unhappily aware that people were watching. "Alcindor, I'll go with you. You don't have to drag me."

"Release the prince," the aide said at once. He fixed his cold gaze on Prince Alexander and said, "The king is waiting. I am glad you have seen fit to listen to reason—for once."

In their private quarters, King Alquin and Queen Lenore listened to Dethenor as he spoke urgently.

"I know that we are apprehensive about the armies of Zor," Dethenor said.

"We are," the king answered. "Do you truly think we can hold them back?"

"For a time. But only for a time. They have many men, and only the excellence of our archers at the passes has kept us safe thus far."

"A long time ago," King Alquin said, "I realized that good archers would be our only protection from the Zorians—since we are so outnumbered. Fortunately, we have the finest archers in NuWorld."

"That is true, Your Majesty, and until now they

have been our salvation. But I must tell you that there are rumors . . ." He paused at that point and looked worried.

"What kind of rumors?" the king demanded.

"They are very vague. But we have heard that the Zorians have developed some sort of secret offense. A weapon, you could call it—perhaps under the direction of the Dark Lord. That would not surprise me."

"A better kind of bow? Our bows are the best that can be made."

"I do not know, Your Majesty. I simply have heard from one of our reliable agents that they have developed *something* that will be difficult for our archers to defend against. I think what we must—" Dethenor broke off as a knock came at the door.

"Come in!" the king called.

It opened, and Alcindor entered, accompanied by an unusually subdued-appearing prince.

"Did he come willingly, Alcindor?" the king asked.

The aide hesitated, and then a small smile turned up the corners of his mouth. "Yes, after he understood the situation, Your Majesty."

"What does this mean, Father?" Alexander asked peevishly. "Why have you had me brought here like a criminal?"

"My orders to Alcindor were to let you know that I wished your presence. If you had obeyed of your own free will, that would have been very simple," the king said sternly.

Alex dropped his head, and Alquin thought a look of shame briefly swept across his son's face.

"Well," the prince muttered, "I'm here. What's the purpose of your summons?"

King Alquin studied his son. He loved the boy

dearly but was afraid that he had failed him as a father. He had been gone to the wars most of Alexander's childhood and had not given him the example he should have. He regretted that now, but there was no way to change what had already happened.

"You are eighteen years old, Alex," the king said. "And I have decided that your life is worthless."

Alexander flushed and straightened up as though he had never been talked to like this before. "I resent that, Father!" he said furiously.

"And I resent the life that you lead! You are a prince, and the kingdom is in grave danger. I have brought you here to tell you that from this point on your life will be different."

"Different! And what does that mean?" Alex demanded.

"There will be no more drinking, no more gambling, no more parties. That bunch of leeches that follows you around, and whom you cannot see for what they are, will be dismissed from the capital. You will become a soldier and endure all the hardness of a soldier."

Alquin saw the rebellion flaring in his son's eyes and was not surprised. The queen herself was silent, but the king continued talking, and he did not soften his words. "You are a disgrace to the royal family, Alex! I am ashamed of you! You are no son of mine until you prove yourself so!"

Prince Alexander might have been wise to bow his head and surrender to the king's demands. But it appeared that a lifetime of getting his own way was going to prevent that. He stood straight and said angrily, "I will do exactly as I please, and you will not treat me as if I were a commoner!"

"Is that your final answer?"

"Yes!"

"Alcindor," King Alquin said, "the prince will be confined to his quarters until further notice. Take him there now. He will receive no visitors; he will not be allowed to leave."

"Wait! You can't do that to me!"

"You will see what a king can do. Take him, Alcindor!"

Alcindor escorted the prince out as Alexander attempted to fight him off. His strength was no match, however, for the strength of the stalwart soldier. The prince's angry voice was still echoing from the hall after the door closed.

Queen Lenore arose then and went to her husband. She stood behind him and put both hands on his shoulders. "Try not to feel too bad, Alquin. It is my fault as much as yours. We both have spoiled him."

Heavily the king nodded. "And what are we to do now?"

The queen hesitated. Then she said firmly, "I think we must send for help."

"Military help? There is none."

"I think our problem is not mostly a military one. It is something else. I think we should send for Goél."

King Alquin lifted his eyes. Thoughts raced through his head. He was heartbroken over the rebellion of his only child. He truly wanted help. And now he whispered, "Yes. Send a courier at once and ask Goél if he will come and help us."

"What sort of visitor are you talking about?"

The servant of Count Ferrod did not answer for a moment. He was a thin man with pale, shifty eyes. "I do not know how to describe him. He is not from here. He has come on a long journey, he says, and he demands to see you."

"What name did he give?"

"He gave no name, but he said Count Ferrod would want to see him."

"Well, show him in."

Ferrod leaned back in his chair and glanced over at his wife. "Who do you suppose *this* is?"

Countess Grenda said, "Probably someone wanting a favor. We get plenty of those."

However, when the door opened and the visitor entered, the count knew that this man had not come to beg favors. He was tall and powerfully built, and the hood that was thrown back from his black cloak revealed a thin, dark, strong face. He gave them a brief time to study him before saying, "My name is Rondel."

"What is your purpose with us—Rondel?"

"I have come to do you a great favor." Rondel had a black mustache and neat black beard. His skin was dead white in contrast, and there was something even dangerous looking about him. Count Ferrod found himself becoming a little uneasy. "Is your business political or personal?"

"Both," Rondel said at once.

"It must be one or the other," the countess snapped. When the man turned his cold gaze on her, she appeared to have a moment of fear. But she quickly recovered and said, "State your purpose or leave us."

"I will indeed do so, Countess." Rondel moved closer, and his voice dropped. "What I have to say is for your ears only. Not even your closest friends or servants must know."

"What can be this mysterious business you have with us?" Ferrod asked curiously.

"The kingdom of Madria is doomed."

"That is treason to speak so!" the count gasped. "You cannot say that!"

"You said as much in the Council this morning, did you not?"

"How did you know what I said in Council?"

"I know many things, but it is not necessary to share with you how I know. What is my purpose? I have come to give you an opportunity to save yourself and to rise above your present position."

Ferrod and his wife exchanged quick glances. "What are you saying, Rondel?"

"I will tell you the truth. I serve the Dark Lord."

A chill passed over the count. He had heard of the Dark Lord of NuWorld. He knew the Dark Lord's power was creeping over the land. He also had heard of the one called Goél, who fought against it. And he knew that the king and queen had, in fact, put their trust in Goél.

"I will not listen to you. It is treason."

"It is wisdom," Rondel said. "The kingdom of Madria cannot stand. Your powers shrink every day, while those of the Dark Lord grow. His shadow is long, and it will grow longer. Soon the mountain passes will be taken. You will look out that window one day and see in the streets the soldiers of Zor, wearing the sign of the Dark Lord on their breasts. Then all will be lost."

"I do not believe it," Ferrod said, but his voice was weak.

"Yes, you do believe it. And I have come to make you an offer from the Dark Lord himself." The dark man smiled suddenly. "I see that interests you. Do you think that he does not know what is in your heart?"

"No one knows what is in my heart."

"No? What about this? If the king dies of his old

wounds and then the prince dies of sickness or disease or in the war, who would be the next king of Madria?"

A silence fell over the room.

"Do not be alarmed. I realize that to speak so would be treason as things now stand, but things will not remain as they are. Give your allegiance to the Dark Lord, and you two will rule over the kingdom. You will be regents of the Dark Lord and have all power—under him."

Rondel talked on. His voice grew soft and steady and tempting. For some time the count and the countess listened to him.

Suddenly the dark stranger asked, "What is your decision?"

Count Ferrod swallowed hard. A question troubled him. "But what of the prince?"

"The prince must not stand in the way of your greatness. He is a fool, and everyone in the kingdom knows it. You are not a fool, Count Ferrod. Neither are you, Countess. You will not throw away what is being offered you on a worthless boy whose only talent is drinking and gambling and partying. Quick! Your answer. I will have it now. For once I leave this room, there will be no chance to change your mind."

At that moment Grenda proved herself to be the stronger of the two. She took her husband's arm, and she whispered, "We must do it, Ferrod. There is no other sensible choice."

Count Ferrod studied his wife's expression, then turned back to their visitor. "All right, Rondel. We accept your offer."

Rondel laughed. "You would be a fool not to. Now, this is what you must do . . ."

3
Josh Loses

Golden sunlight spread over the emerald green waters, and white sand surrounded the inlet like a ring. Josh Adams came up from a deep dive, expelled his breath, brushed his hair out of his eyes, and then bobbed in the warm waters.

Suddenly, Sarah Collingwood shot up next to him and splashed water into his face.

"Watch what you're doing, Sarah!" Josh protested. He reached out to duck her, but to his surprise she abruptly disappeared. The next thing he knew, he felt two hands close on his ankles, and he shouted, "Hey!" and then was jerked under.

Kicking himself free, Josh came to the surface, sputtering and spitting out the salty water.

Sarah came up laughing, a few feet away. At four-teen, exactly the same age as Josh, she was small and very pretty. Josh was tall, and he considered himself gangling and awkward. He hated being spindly, he hated being clumsy, and especially he hated being best-ed in anything by Sarah Collingwood.

Josh and Sarah had been friends for years. Even before a nuclear war had wrecked the earth and turned it into NuWorld, they had known each other. They had awakened from their sleep capsules to find the world they knew gone forever. NuWorld was filled with strange beasts, and the geography was completely altered. Josh had soon found himself leading the young people known as the Seven Sleepers, under the direction of their mentor Goél. They were engaged in a war. It was to keep the Dark Lord from enslaving the inhabitants of Nu-World.

Sarah looked back at the shore where the other five Sleepers were playing with a kind of beach ball. "Race you to the beach, Josh," she challenged, her eyes sparkling.

Josh treaded water, trying to think of some way to get out of the challenge. He knew that Sarah was a better swimmer, just as she was a better archer. In fact, Sarah was better at almost everything than Josh Adams was. Usually he tried to avoid a contest with her, but now he saw there was no escape.

"All right," he said.

"Well, we have to make it a real challenge. What does the winner get?"

"I don't know," Josh said. He just wanted to get the race over with.

"I'll tell you what," Sarah answered. "The loser has to cook supper and serve the winner and everyone else at the table tonight."

Josh hated moments like this. Thinking to gain a little edge, he suddenly kicked vigorously and threw himself into a stroke, yelling, "All right!" He put his head down, his legs thrashed the water, and he swam as hard as he could.

For a time, he even thought he might win. He had gotten a good start while Sarah was still getting ready. But then he saw that she was already pulling alongside. Another glance revealed that she was swimming steadily, doing a fine stroke, turning to take a breath of air every third stroke, and expelling it underwater. She swam smoothly and apparently without effort. As always.

Josh tried to imitate her. But suddenly, instead of

expelling air, he made a mistake and strangled as water ran up his nose. He floundered around, spitting and blinking, and by the time he got started again, he saw that all was lost.

Sarah reached the beach several strokes ahead of him, pulled herself up, and stood waiting. "Where have you been, slowpoke? You must have taken a shortcut by way of China."

Josh was disgusted with himself. He stalked up the beach toward the rest of the Sleepers, his back rigid with anger.

Sarah followed him, and, when they reached the others, of course she had to call out cheerfully, "Guess what? Josh has agreed to cook supper and serve us tonight. Isn't that wonderful?"

"I think it's peachy!" The speaker was Jake Garfield, a thirteen-year-old with red hair and a pug nose. He punched Josh on the shoulder. "Mighty noble of you, Josh. I didn't know you had it in you."

Josh glared at him and pulled away.

Dave Cooper, fifteen and handsome with crisp brown hair, was the oldest of the Sleepers. He winked at Sarah and said, "What did you do to make him agree to do that?"

Perhaps Sarah saw that Josh's feelings were hurt and did not want to shame him further. She just said, "Oh, Josh likes to do things for us. You know that, Dave."

"I never caught him at it." Dave shrugged. "But if you say so."

Abbey, the fourteen-year-old blonde with blue eyes, was lying on her back, sunning. Back in OldWorld she had been intending to become the winner of a beauty contest, perhaps even Miss America. But in

NuWorld there were no beauty contests. Instead there were dragons and fierce people and the Dark Lord. She raised her head from the sand and said, "Make my steak medium rare, will you, Josh?" Then she lay back and ignored everybody.

The remaining two Sleepers were a contrast. Reb Jackson was a tall fourteen-year-old with sandy hair and light blue eyes. He was burned by the sun and looked strong and athletic. He elbowed the small boy next to him and said, "What do you think, Wash? You think we should give old Josh a hand?"

Gregory Randolph Washington Jones, twelve, was the youngest of the Sleepers. He flashed a toothy smile at his big friend and said, "I guess so." Then he said to Josh, "Sure. We'll give you a hand, Josh."

"I don't need a hand!" Josh snapped crossly. "I said I'd cook the supper and serve everybody, and I will!"

"Well, you don't have to bite his head off," Reb said with some irritation. "He was just trying to help."

Josh did not answer. Usually he was a very amiable young man, but Sarah had beaten him—again— and besides, he felt unqualified to be the leader of the Sleepers, anyway. Others, such as Dave and Abbey, were smarter. Jake could fix anything mechanical. Reb was an expert horseman, an expert with a rope. Wash could cook. Everyone could do something better than he could, and Josh had never understood why Goél had made him the leader in the first place.

He marched on back to the cabin where they had been staying for the past two weeks, muttering, "All right, I'll fix supper. I can't cook as good as Wash, but I'll do the best I can if it kills me."

The Sleepers were on a rare vacation. They had just come through an exhausting adventure, and Goél had sent them here for a welcome rest. The ocean was just the place, and they had been enjoying the sandy beach, the swimming, the fishing.

As Josh entered the cabin and began preparing supper, he knew that he was behaving miserably. "I don't know why I act like that," he muttered. "I ought to be zapped." Sometimes he simply could not throw off these bad moods.

He worked hard on the supper, having decided it would include baked potatoes, carrots, corn on the cob, and juicy steaks.

When the meal was finally ready, he walked to the door and stuck his head out. "Come and get it!" he yelled.

Immediately all the other Sleepers began rapidly coming toward the cabin. They filed in and washed their hands. When they sat down at the table, Wash said, "Mmmm! Sure does smell good!"

"Nice to have a servant to wait on us, too." Dave grinned, winking across the table at Abbey. "I think you've found your calling, Josh. I vote that we let Josh do all the cooking from now on. And he's a natural-born waiter besides."

Josh glared. He had always envied Dave his good looks and his athletic ability, and now Dave's teasing cut him.

Sarah glanced at his face. "I'll help with the serv-ing, Josh," she said quickly.

"No, I lost the race, and I'll pay the penalty," Josh said shortly.

Josh's meal turned out to be all right. The steaks were properly done, the corn was tender, and the car-rots and the potatoes were steaming hot. The only problem was the scowl on his face. Dave made it worse by continuing to needle him until Sarah murmured, "Dave, please be quiet!"

"I was only teasing," Dave protested.

"Well, you've teased enough, so hush."

At that moment the door swung open. They all looked up, and every one of them let out an exclamation of surprise.

"Goél!" Sarah cried, her eyes sparkling. She jumped up and hurried to meet him.

The newcomer took her hands and looked down at her. "How are you, my daughter?"

Goél was a mysterious figure. He had strange powers. But he was good, and the Sleepers had learned to trust him for help and advice. He was a tall man with light brown hair and dark, deep-set eyes. His skin was tanned to a golden sheen, and he wore a simple gray robe with the hood thrown back.

The Sleepers were all on their feet by now, and Goél went around the room greeting each of them. Josh was last, and Goél said, "Well, Josh, and how are you enjoying your vacation?"

"OK," Josh said gruffly. For some reason he felt embarrassed in Goél's presence. "Why don't you sit down, sire, and I'll bring you something to eat?"

Goél's dark eyes studied him. He knew Josh was upset. How did he know that?

"It appears that you have been the cook today, Josh," Goél said. "Let us do this—you sit down now, and I'll serve *you*."

Josh was shocked. "Oh, no, that wouldn't be right!"

"Now do as I say," Goél said. "Here, make Josh a place. All of you sit down and continue your meal, while I grill my good friend Josh Adams a nice steak. How do you like it, Josh?"

"Uh . . . medium well," Josh murmured.

Goél busied himself at the stove. All the while, he kept up a steady stream of conversation, asking them about their vacation and what they had been doing. He even told them some of the activities that were going on in other parts of NuWorld.

When Josh's steak was ready, Goél set it before him, saying, "There. I hope you like it."

"But you don't have to serve me, sire," Josh protested again. "You are special. I ought to be waiting on *you*—because of who you are."

Goél put his hand on Josh's shoulder. "Remember, I've always said that true greatness is connected with serving. The truly special are not those who are waited on, but those who give themselves to helping others. What I have done will remind you all in days to come." He continued to speak for some time about serving others. Then Goél laughed and said, "But enough of the sermon. Now I'll have some of this good food myself."

They continued eating and talking, and when all were finished, Goél leaned forward and folded his hands on the table. "That was fine," he said. Then he silently looked around, studying each face.

When Goél looked at people, Josh thought, it seemed he entered into their thinking. All the Sleepers said that. It was a peculiar thing. When they had a clear conscience, they could face him, and it was a pleasure. But when they had been involved in some activity that they knew would not please Goél, it was almost impossible to hold his gaze. Josh felt that way when his turn came.

But after looking each in the eyes, Goél smiled. "I imagine it wouldn't be too hard for you to guess what I'm doing here."

"I reckon not," Reb spoke up. "You've got another job for us to do."

"That's right, Reb. I must interrupt your rest. Maybe someday I'll come and not bring a hard task—but I'm afraid this time I do."

Sarah said quickly, "We don't mind, Goél. That's what we're here for. What mission is it this time?"

"There is a kingdom called Madria. It's approximately a five days' journey from here. The king and queen are faithful servants of mine, and they are in considerable difficulty." He looked thoughtful. "They are surrounded by enemies. The nearby kingdom of Zor is occupied by savage people under the influence of the Dark Lord, who have been at war with Madria for some time. Now I fear that unless something happens, Madria will be lost."

"What is it exactly you would like for us to do?" Josh asked, forgetting his bad mood for a moment.

"One thing that must be done," Goél said, "concerns the young prince of Madria. His name is Alexander. He has taken a wrong turn in his life, and I would ask you to do what you can to change his ways."

"How old is he, Goél?" Sarah asked.

"He is eighteen years old and a very fine looking young man." He smiled at Abbey, saying, "I wish that he were as fine inside as he is outside."

"What's wrong with him, sire?" Wash asked.

"Unfortunately, he has been pampered all of his life. He is an only child, so perhaps it's understandable, but Alexander's parents made a sad and grievous error. It isn't good for a young man—or a young woman—to have his own way all the time.

"In any case," Goél went on, "King Alquin was a splendid soldier indeed, and as long as he was able to lead, I did not concern myself with Zor's overrunning Madria. But now things are different. The king was severely wounded in the wars and is not well. It will soon be time for Prince Alexander to step into his father's place, but I fear he is unprepared."

"Well, what can we do to help?" Jake spoke up. "We can't *make* him do the right thing."

"I do not think anyone can ever force another to 'do the right thing.' But by now you have had some experience with people, and you have all learned some things yourselves." He suddenly looked at Josh and said abruptly, "I mentioned a moment ago that serving is the most important element of greatness. Prince Alexander needs to learn to forget himself and to serve his parents and his country. If you can teach him that, I think all will be well."

The Sleepers sat silent, thinking.

At last Sarah said quietly, "We will do all we can, Goél, to help the people of Madria."

Goél too had fallen quiet. Now he roused himself, and his expression took on a touch of sadness. "I think Prince Alexander has come to a crossroads. Either he will grow up and become a man of honor and valor like his father, or he will become something quite different. I trust that you will help him to take the right path."

4

The Spoiled Brat

The Sleepers pressed their horses hard, and the journey was tiring. They paused each day at noon for a break, then rode until almost dark. Now they rode their weary animals through the territory of Zor, and Josh sensed that everyone was apprehensive.

"This is a spooky place," Jake muttered. He was not a good rider and had been thrown more than once. He often looked with envy at Reb, who rode his tall, roan stallion easily.

Reb looked about at the rising countryside and shrugged his shoulders. "Not such a bad looking place, I'd say."

"Country's not bad," Jake snapped back, "but the people here aren't much!"

In truth, as they had passed through the kingdom of Zor, they had found the people to be sullen and unfriendly. They were a brown-skinned people, burned by the sun, and most of the men wore black beards. They kept their beards oiled, and that somehow gave them a rather evil appearance.

At the head of the small party of travelers, Josh kept his eyes moving from point to point. Late in the day, he spotted something troubling. "Look ahead, Sarah. I think that's some sort of military group up there."

Sarah looked in the direction that Josh indicated. "They're soldiers all right. A lot of them."

"Well, I hope they don't give us any trouble."

They rode up to where a unit of heavily armed Zorian troops had formed themselves into a line. The soldiers' eyes glittered, and several of them had arrows notched into their bows, ready to shoot.

"Halt! What's your business here?"

The speaker was a burly man. He seemed to be an officer, for he wore a four-pointed star on his forehead.

"We're travelers," Josh said, "making our way through to Madria."

At the name of their destination the muscular officer examined them even more closely, and a mutter went down the line of soldiers. Now all the warriors were fingering their swords or their bows ominously.

"What is your business in Madria?"

"We have private business there." Josh reached into an inner pocket and pulled forth a sheet of parchment. "We have safe passage here from the Zorian minister himself."

Another mutter went up and down the line, and the officer snatched at the paper. He studied it, peering at it closely, and then growled. "It appears to be in order." Handing the sheet back, he examined the riders one more time. Apparently he decided that these strangers were not a threat, for he laughed harshly and said, "When you get to Madria, tell them their days are just about over."

Josh did not answer the Zorian, not wanting to antagonize him. Instead he nodded, stuck the pass back into his pocket, and kicked his horse into a swift gallop.

The others followed, and soon all were at the crest of the mountain. It was a high mountain and studded with deep green forest, trees so thick that it was not easy to make their way through.

Josh looked around him and said, "From what I understand, these mountains are all that save Madria from being overwhelmed by the Zorians. There are only a few passes that can be traveled. I expect we'll be running into the Madrian border guards pretty soon."

He was not wrong. Within five minutes, they encountered another detachment of soldiers. These were taller men and not so heavy as the Zorians. The man who came forward to meet them was wearing a light green uniform and was backed with a dozen other soldiers wearing the same. These troops too carried bows and arrows held at the ready.

"Halt!"

Josh reined in his horse at once and threw up his hands. As the other horses drew up behind him, he said, "My name is Josh Adams. My companions and I seek an audience with the king of Madria."

"Many people seek an audience with the king. We don't allow every traveler that happens to ask for it such an audience."

But Josh had come prepared for this. He reached into his pocket again, found an envelope, and handed it to the officer. "Here is a letter signed by the king himself requesting our presence. I think he will be glad to see us."

The officer's eyes swept the writing, and then he handed back the letter. "Very well. If you will follow me, I will take you to the king myself." He turned to the soldiers and said, "Keep close guard. Framan, take charge until I return."

The Sleepers and their guide started off, and the officer gave Josh a curious look more than once. Finally he observed, "Not many people are able to travel through Zor to reach our country."

"We had a pass signed by the minister of Zor himself."

"That must be quite a trick. He doesn't give those out every day."

Josh could tell that the soldier was bursting with curiosity. But he thought it best not to reveal anything further, and he kept his silence until they had reached the capital.

"I don't see many people on the streets," Josh said.

The officer said—rather sadly, Josh thought—"No. Our numbers are not what they were."

Sarah was riding close to Josh as they made their way along the narrow streets. What people there were looked harried and worn.

"The people look so *tired*," she murmured. "It must be the ongoing war that Goél told us about."

"They don't look too good," Josh agreed. "From what I understand, they've had a hard time of it and are on the brink of being wiped out by the Zorians."

The soldier led them to a palace made of reddish stone. It stretched up toward the sky, and its windows were all barred. "Visitors to see the king," their guide announced. "They have a letter from His Majesty himself."

A big, well-built man wearing a dark green uniform and a helmet made of silver said, "I will see to it. How go things at the front?"

"As always," the officer said gloomily. He turned his weary animal around and headed back for the front lines.

"I will have your horses cared for," the guard said. "My name is Dreban. I will take you to the king at once."

Josh slipped off his horse and found that his legs were aching and numb from the long ride. He glanced with envy at Reb, who hopped off his mount as cheerfully and easily as if he had made only a half-hour's ride.

The Sleepers followed the soldier through the gates. When they entered the palace, Josh was impressed with the beauty of it all. There were carvings of white ivory everywhere, and beautiful statues rested on high pedestals. All of the palace help were clothed in dark green. A beautiful curving staircase took them to the second floor. From time to time the walls were broken with long, narrow, barred windows. Guards were posted at almost every door.

And then their soldier came to a double door. He nodded at the two guards, who stepped aside, and he knocked. He waited for a moment, and then the door opened. "Visitors from outside, sir," he announced. "They have a letter from the king himself."

The old man who had answered the door stepped back. "Come in," he said. He waited until the Seven Sleepers had entered, then said, "My name is Dethenor. I am master of the High Council of the king."

Josh produced the king's letter, and Dethenor studied it. At once he said, "You are welcome here. You come at a needy time."

"On the way, we passed through the land of Zor. They seem to be preparing for a new attack."

"Indeed they are," Dethenor said wearily. "We are in a dreary time." Then the old man brightened. "But come. I will take you to the king and the queen. They will welcome your presence."

Josh and the others followed the old man, and he led them through several large rooms. Finally he stood briefly at a carved door before opening it. "The king is not well," he said. "We must not disturb him for long."

"Of course not, sir. We would not wish to do that."

When they entered, Josh saw that the king was resting on a kind of couch. It had a back that supported him. His face was kind but lined with pain. Beside him an older woman stood, one of the most beautiful that Josh had ever seen.

"King Alquin and Queen Lenore, I present to you our visitors. You may introduce yourselves."

Josh stepped forward and bowed deeply. "Your Majesty and Queen Lenore, I am Josh Adams." He named the other Sleepers and then said, "We have been asked by our master, Goél, to lend you what assistance we can."

The king and queen exchanged smiles, and then King Alquin turned his eyes back to study his young visitors. "The Seven Sleepers. Indeed, we had asked Goél for help, and we are grateful to him for sending you. We have heard of your exploits."

"Perhaps if you would tell us the problem," Josh said, "we can make some plans."

"The problem is not difficult to explain," the king said wearily. He went on to tell about the long war between his country and Zor. "We are ringed in here by mountains, and the mountains have protected us. But the Zorians are wearing us down. They are a larger people than we, and it takes all of our strength simply to keep them fought off."

"Have you considered attacking?" Josh asked. "It seems to me you give them the advantage by just sitting here and waiting for them to 'wear you down.'"

"That was my plan until I was wounded," the king said. "Things were going well, but since that time we have made no progress."

Josh and the other Sleepers listened as the king explained further.

Then Josh said, "It still seems to me, sire, that your only hope is in attack. Perhaps cutting through the lines and establishing a base outside so that you can keep the Zorians away from the mountain passes?"

"That would require great skill and a great leader —which we do not have." Queen Lenore spoke quietly. "As long as my husband was at the head of the army, such a thing was possible. But now I'm afraid we cannot count on that."

"What about your son? I understand he is old enough to be a warrior."

At once the king lowered his eyes, and the queen seemed to flinch. Josh glanced at Dethenor, and the old man shook his head slightly.

It was the queen who said, "We may as well be honest with you. You have come to help us, and the truth is always best. Our son, Alexander, has been a disappointment to us. He has taken no interest in his responsibilities to the kingdom, and he spends his time only in pleasure."

Josh saw that the admission hurt the queen, and he said quickly, "It takes longer for some young people to grow up than others, Your Highness. Perhaps he is right on the verge. In any case, our master, Goél, indicated that we should try to be an encouragement to your son."

An eager look came into the queen's eyes. "Did he especially ask you to do that? If you could only stir Alexander to an effort, it would make such a difference. Our people need kingly leadership."

"True," King Alquin said. "I'm not growing any younger, and my wounds are grievous. Talk to our son. Encourage him. See what you can do. He is really our only hope."

"We will do our best." Josh bowed. "If you will have someone take us to the prince—"

"We do not have a happy situation," Queen Lenore said. "He is being held in his room now because of his arrogant behavior toward his father. But you certainly may see him. I will go with you and inform the guards that you are to be admitted at any time."

The Seven Sleepers all bowed, and they left the room with the queen.

Queen Lenore led them up two more flights and down a long, ornate hallway. Two guards stood at what seemed to be the prince's door. "Any of these young people are to be admitted into the quarters of the prince at any time," the queen told them.

"Yes, Your Highness," one said at once.

She turned back to the Sleepers. "I can only hope that you will find a way to soften his heart."

Josh said, "Your Majesty, I was thinking as we walked up here—it might be a bit too much if all seven of us descend upon Prince Alexander at once. Perhaps only Sarah and I should visit him just now."

"That is wisely said. Meantime, I will take your friends to your quarters."

As the others moved on down the hall, Joshua nodded to the guards. "I think we'd like to go in now."

A guard knocked on the door, then opened it. He called out, "Two visitors for you, my prince."

Josh and Sarah entered and saw by the window a tall young man with thick, long auburn hair. He had a well-shaped face and blue eyes. He was perhaps a little heavy, but he looked strong and fit.

"Who are you, and what do you want?"

"My name is Josh Adams, and this is Sarah Collingwood, Prince Alexander."

"What is your business with me?" the prince asked coldly.

Sarah spoke up. "We have come at the request of your father. He sent a letter to Goél for help, and Goél sent us. Are you familiar with him?"

"Of course. My parents serve him, and I suppose I will someday." Prince Alexander stared at them, and puzzlement came to his eyes. "But why would my father send for *children?* I can understand sending for soldiers to fight. But what good can you do?"

Josh almost asked, "What good are *you* doing?" but he bit his tongue while Sarah answered. "We have been able to help others from time to time. You may have heard of the Seven Sleepers . . ."

Recognition came to the young prince's eyes, and he grunted. At that moment a small dog bounced barking into the room from an opposite doorway. She was a golden-haired dog with bright eyes. The prince picked her up. "Be quiet, Shasta," he said, stroking her silky fur. Then he nodded slightly. "Yes. I have heard of the Seven Sleepers. Tall tales, I've always thought, about fighting with monsters and winning battles. I can't believe two such as you could do much of that."

Josh suddenly decided that straight talk might be the best in this case. "My prince, I must speak to you in a most open manner. Part of the reason we are here is that you have not fulfilled your responsibilities."

Anger leaped into the eyes of Prince Alexander then, and he snapped. "It's none of your business what I do or what I don't do!"

"It's the business of your father and your mother. It's the business of the Council and the business of all of your people. They are all depending on you, and, unfortunately, you have not been dependable."

41

"Get out of here!" the prince shouted. He walked toward the door, carrying the small dog in one arm and muttering under his breath.

Sarah followed him, pleading, "Prince, just listen to reason. We truly just want to help." She spoke for some time, but Josh could see that she was doing no good. Finally she lost her temper. "You call yourself a prince? You're a spoiled brat!"

The prince turned on her so quickly that his long hair whirled. Again he yelled, "Get out of here!" Then he opened the door and said, "Guard, take these people out!"

"You don't have to do this," Josh said rather sadly. "Think it over, prince. Your country needs you. It's no time to sit up in a tower and pout."

"I've heard enough from you both. Now get *out!*"

As soon as they were down the hall and out of hearing of the guards, Josh said bitterly, "There's no help for him. He's worthless."

Sarah did not answer for a moment, but then she said quietly, "There's hope for everybody, Josh. And I did wrong to get angry. There's hope for everybody."

5
The Cost of a Crown

Sarah drew the bow to full strength. She held it there for two seconds, standing as still as a statue carved out of rock. Then she released the string. It slapped the gauntlet on her left arm, and she heard the arrow as it whizzed through the air. It flew straight and true, and, as always, she felt a thrill when it struck the center of the target with a solid *clunk*.

"A fine shot, Sarah!" Alcindor stood to her left, nodding his approval. His piercing gray eyes were warm as he said, "You are a fine archer! I have seldom seen better."

Sarah flushed at the praise, and again she admired the tall form of the friendly aide. Alcindor seemed such a fine young man, and the thought came to her, *How much better it would be if he were the king's son, instead of that Alexander!* She certainly did not say this aloud, however. She stepped back to let Alcindor take his turn.

He drew a heavy bow with a much stronger pull than Sarah's, and she watched as he loosed the shaft. It did not quite strike the center of the target, but the power of the large bow and his strong arm drove it in up to the feathers.

"Not dead center like yours."

"But if it had been an enemy, that would have made no difference," Sarah replied. "You place great importance on archery here in Madria."

"It has been our salvation," Alcindor said. "That

and the mountains." He rested the tip of the bow on the toe of his sandal, and his eyes grew serious. "We are not a numerous people, and we could not meet an army with swords. We would be overwhelmed. So every Madrian begins to draw a bow almost before he can walk. It is the national sport and pastime here as well as our chief means of defense."

"I've seen some of the younger ones practicing. Almost like babies with tiny bows. They take great pride in it, don't they?"

Alcindor nodded. "Yes, indeed." His face clouded over then. "I wish you had brought with you a thousand as good with a bow as yourself, Sarah."

"Perhaps that would not have been best. It's well for people to fight for their own liberties, don't you think, Alcindor?"

"I do agree. But still, we are hard-pressed here, and what I wouldn't give for at least a hundred good, strong archers—like yourself. Your companions—I perceive they are not as good with a bow as you are . . ."

Sarah was embarrassed. "I may be a little better than some of them, but they are all good at other things. Jake, for instance, can invent anything you want. He can shoe a horse, make a knife—anything like that. And Reb, he is a horseman such as there never was. He could ride anything on four feet."

Alcindor listened as Sarah sang the praises of her companions. He said, "You are a modest young lady, and I honor you for it."

"Alcindor, what was the prince like as he was growing up? You knew him when he was younger, didn't you? You're about the same age."

"Know him? I grew up with him. We were raised together. My father was one of the king's most faithful warriors. So we were put together when we were very young."

"Then what was he like when he was growing up?"

Alcindor gave Sarah an odd stare. "Why do you ask this, Sarah?"

"Well, I hate to say anything bad about the prince, but he doesn't seem very interested in assuming his responsibilities."

"Unfortunately, you are right."

"Was he always as . . . as self-centered as he is now?"

"Indeed, no! I truly don't know how he came to be what he is. He was always warmhearted, generous, and very able. If he were to give himself to being a soldier and leader the way he gives himself to following pleasure, he would make a fine king indeed."

"What do you suppose happened to him?"

"Who can say?"

"But something must have."

"I can't put my finger on it. Until he was through boyhood, he was as fine a boy as you would want to find. But when he came into young manhood, perhaps he began to listen to the praises of the people around him. The wrong people. They wanted things from him, and they flattered him in order to get what they wanted. And they taught him to follow gambling, drinking, partying. I tried to talk to him, but he just laughed at me. Everyone has tried."

Sarah stroked her bow for a moment, thinking. Then she did say, quietly, "I believe you are more a son to the king than Alexander."

"I am not of the royal family," Alcindor said at once very firmly. "The people want a king of royal blood—as well as one who will fight for them." The sorrow that

Sarah had seen in Alcindor before was again reflected in his eyes. "I do not know if we will ever see that man."

Dave and Abbey went for a walk outside the palace and for some time wandered about the grounds, admiring them. They had just come from a visit with Prince Alexander. Josh had suggested that all the Sleepers, at one time or another, attempt to win the confidence of the young prince.

As they strolled along, Dave said, "I don't know what to make of him, Abbey."

"Isn't he the handsomest thing!" she exclaimed. "That hair! Any girl would envy it!"

"Well, he may have beautiful hair, but you can't get around one thing— he's sulking."

Abbey, who usually hated to say anything bad about anyone, tried to defend the prince. "He just needs time to grow up."

"Time to grow up! He's eighteen years old. He's a man. He's had plenty of time to grow up."

"He's *physically* grown up, but—well, I've got confidence that someday he'll be the kind of man on the inside that he should be."

Dave walked on beside Abbey. He knew she was impressed with good looks more than she should be. After a while he said, "I know a lot about sulking, Abbey. I've done some of it in my day. Haven't you?"

Abbey made a face at him. She started to answer but then nodded toward the stranger walking up to the palace door. "Wonder who that is, Dave. He doesn't look like he belongs here."

Dave did not mind asking questions. They were passing a guard, who greeted them, and Dave said, "Say, soldier, who is that man going inside? Do you know?”

The guard, a short man with a round face and guileless blue eyes, said, “His name is Rondel.”

“Is he one of you? He belongs here?”

“Oh no. He’s a foreigner. He came to the palace a little while ago—on business, perhaps. No one knows much about him.”

“What sort of business?”

“It’s not for me to know that.”

“Is he a friend of the king?”

“Not that I know of. He’s a friend of Count Ferrod and the countess, though. I believe he comes to see them.”

“Thanks for the information.” Dave walked on with Abbey. “For some reason, I don’t like the looks of that fellow.”

“I don’t, either,” Abbey said. “He looks like . . . something evil.”

Rondel entered the reception room of Count Ferrod. He waited until the attendant closed the door, then said without another moment’s hesitation, “Things are going badly. I’m disappointed.”

“We’re doing all we can, Rondel,” Count Ferrod said. “What do you expect?”

Rondel did not answer that question. Instead, he asked another. “When did these Sleepers come here?”

“Just a few days ago. What about them?”

“The Dark Lord is their deadly enemy, and they are his!”

“They are only children,” the countess said. “They are no danger to anyone.”

“Others have said that before and learned to their sorrow that these so-called ‘children’ are more deadly than they seem.”

"I can't believe that!" Ferrod exclaimed. "They are not even out of their midteens!"

"Power is not always a matter of years. Some old men have no power at all. These 'children,' as you call them, are the servants of Goél."

"Servants of Goél! I didn't know that," Ferrod said, looking shocked.

"The Dark Lord would find it *acceptable* if they were put to death."

Now both the count and the countess appeared shocked by his words. Ferrod said, "We would have no reason for that . . ."

"That would be up to you to find. I will say that the Dark Lord would be pleased if they were all sunk in the deepest pit with tons of rocks on top of them."

The count and the countess were silent for a moment. At last she said, "What will happen next, Rondel?"

He stared at the two of them as if weighing them in the balances and then said, "The prince is your enemy as well."

"Our enemy! How can that be?" the count cried.

"The king is obviously too ill to lead his people. Perhaps, hopefully, he never will be able. I do not think he will live long. But if he dies, the crown will go to Prince Alexander."

"Of course. That is our way."

"He is a worthless infant, and everyone knows it. He would ruin the kingdom in six months."

"I have always said that," the countess spoke up. "He is not fit to rule."

"But he will rule," Rondel said, "unless you take steps."

"What kind of steps?" the countess asked, her eyes fixed on their visitor.

"The prince must die. If he is dead, the way to the throne will be open to you. You are the only male relative, Count Ferrod. You must court the elders of the Great Council. They must be willing to support you."

"Dethenor will never do that. He hates me," the count said.

"Then it might be well if he too were to disappear."

"You mean—have him assassinated?"

Rondel lost his patience. "This is a *war*, Ferrod! Don't you understand that? Men die in wars. Women die. Even children."

He glared at them, and a silence fell over the room. He watched the countess more closely than he did the count. "Get rid of him," he whispered. "Use poison if you must. Make it look like some sort of illness."

Ferrod turned pale and did not answer, but the countess suddenly straightened up. A glitter came to her eyes, and she said, "It shall be done."

As Rondel gazed at her, an agreement seemed to pass between them. Without another word, he whirled and left the room.

As soon as their visitor was gone, the countess went to her husband. She put an arm around him, and he turned his gaze to meet hers.

"If you would be king," she whispered, "you must be willing to pay the price."

"But to do away with the prince—"

"The cost of the crown is high. Do you want to be king or not?"

"You know that I do."

The countess took a deep breath. "Then put this matter into my hands, and all will come out well."

6

The Tray

The clanging of swords filled the hall, as the two fencers moved about the floor. Their blades made flashes of light like lightning. Back and forth they went.

As the contest went on, Alcindor was impressed by the swordsmanship of the boy before him. He had tried all of the Sleepers, to test their mettle with a sword, and had found that Jake and Wash were mediocre. He decided that the girls were worthless, not having the strength to wield the heavy sword he preferred. Dave was very good, Josh not so expert. But this young man with the red hair and the freckles that stood out on his pale face was holding his own against the best swordsman in Madria.

Suddenly Alcindor threw himself forward and risked everything on a single stroke. But he miscalculated the speed of his opponent. He found his blade turned away, and all at once the beaded point of Reb's sword was on his chest.

"A touch!" Alcindor cried out. "I do confess." He saluted Reb with his blade and then put his arm around the boy's shoulder. "You are a fine swordsman! As good with a sword as Sarah is with a bow."

"Aw, shucks!" Reb said. "I'm not all that good." His eyes were warm and friendly and admiring. "But you were really something, Alcindor. I never saw better."

"You must have had much sword practice almost from the time you were born."

"No, never had a sword in my hand before I came to NuWorld. But I've had to use one a lot since then."

Josh had been watching Reb and Alcindor and found himself to be somewhat envious. He waited until Reb left and then walked over to the king's military aide. "Reb's the best of us with a sword, Alcindor."

"He's a fine swordsman indeed. You must be very proud of him."

"I'm proud of all the Sleepers," Josh told him. Then he sighed. "I'm the only one that's not much good for anything."

"Why would you say a foolish thing like that?"

"But it's true," Josh said. "I can't invent things like Jake. I can't ride a horse or wield a sword like Reb. I can't use a bow like Sarah . . ."

Alcindor smiled. "Still, Goél thought you could do something."

"What do you mean?"

"He made you the leader of the Sleepers, didn't he?"

"Yes, he did, but—"

"If he made you the leader, he saw something in you that perhaps is not obvious to other people—or to yourself. You know, Josh, there are qualities more important than swordsmanship and archery in a kingdom. I have known kings who were not skilled in these things, yet they were always victors. Some individuals have the ability to be leaders when they are not particularly good at other things. I believe you may be one of those."

Josh was embarrassed at the praise. He scuffed his feet in the dirt and decided to change the subject. "What do you think is going to happen in this war, Alcindor?"

The question obviously troubled the tall soldier.

He bit his lip for a moment, then slowly raised his sword and looked along its silvery length. "Nothing good," he admitted finally. "I keep hearing rumors of a new attack. The Zorians are moving their men around in large numbers."

"They've always done that, haven't they?"

"True enough, but this time I hear something else."

"What is it you hear?"

"I've heard from another good authority that the Zorians now have a new weapon."

Josh was interested. "Jake will want to hear about that. Maybe it's a catapult."

"No. Catapults wouldn't do them any good here. They wouldn't help them get through the mountain passes. And that's our secret, Josh. We can hold the passes because we're the best archers *and* we're in a good defensive position. If we ever lost the passes, the Zorians would be in on us like wolves."

"But you're really worried about this, aren't you?"

"Yes, I am. Things do not look good for my country right now."

"We keep hoping that the prince will change and be some help for you."

"You keep on hoping that, Josh." Alcindor tried to smile. "I've hoped for a long time, but nothing has come of it."

Sarah had not really wanted to visit the prince. She had been to see him twice since she and Josh made their initial visit, and both times had been unpleasant. For the most part he simply disregarded her and played with his dog, Shasta. Today she had come to make another try.

"Prince, I know you get tired of me—" she began patiently.

"That's right. I do. I'm tired of you right now. Why don't you go?"

Sarah ignored this. She watched as he ruffled the silky hair of the small dog and tried again. "You must get tired of staying in this room."

"Of course I do. Do you think I'm a fool?"

"Then why don't you get out of it?"

The prince put down the dog and came to stand over her. "Because I'm not a child. I can make up my own mind about what to do with my life."

"But you shouldn't be angry with your father, Prince Alex," Sarah said. "He's one of the finest men I've ever known."

For a moment the prince hesitated, then he said, "He has been a fine soldier and a fine king. He has not been a good father."

"You're angry with him because he wasn't there when you were growing up. But the people of Madria need you, Prince Alex."

"I don't want to talk about it," the prince said. He began to pace around the room, and it was obvious to Sarah that he was indeed sick of his surroundings. He walked to the window and stared out without saying a word. Then he turned back. "The people don't need me. They have Alcindor. He's a first-rate soldier."

"But they are accustomed to having a king at their head, aren't they?"

Reluctantly Alex nodded. "Yes, they are."

"And that will soon be you. *You* are the one who should be out leading the people even now."

Alexander clamped his jaws together and stood staring out the window again. The silence grew until a knock came at the door. Whirling around, he yelled, "Come in!"

The door opened, and a man entered, a small pale-faced man wearing the castle uniform. "A special treat for you from the kitchen, Prince."

Alexander walked over to him and stared down at the tray. It held breads and silver goblets and a silver pitcher.

"Who are you? I haven't seen you before, have I?"

"I am new to the castle service, sire."

"All right. Get out."

"Yes, sire."

The little man scurried out, and the door closed behind him.

Alexander glanced at Sarah. "You might as well eat this. They feed me well enough here, and I'm not hungry."

He poured some wine out of the pitcher into the two goblets. "I guess they knew I had a visitor. Here. Have some of this wine."

"Not for me," Sarah said. "But thank you."

"Suit yourself." The prince picked up his goblet and walked to the window to look out again, silently holding the silver cup.

Sarah joined him there. "It's a beautiful day. Oh, look, they're practicing archery over there."

"I saw you the other day with Alcindor. You're very good. Where did you learn bowmanship?"

"I've always liked archery."

The prince studied her. "Tell me about some of the battles you've been in." He set down the goblet on the windowsill.

Sarah hesitated, then thought, *At least he's talking. Perhaps this is a good way to gain his confidence.*

"Well, there was the time we were engaged in a battle with dinosaurs."

"What are dinosaurs? Here, sit down."

They sat in chairs by the window, and Sarah briefly told the story of when she and the other Sleepers had been trapped in a land where there were dinosaur-like creatures. He listened intently and, to her surprise, asked that she tell another one.

When she finished, he said slowly, "You've certainly had a more adventurous life than I have—and done more good, too, I suppose."

Sarah said, "We try to help wherever we can." She did not want to make much of herself, but she spoke warmly of the other Sleepers.

The prince finally reached for the drink he had set down on the windowsill and said, "Well, here's to you, Sarah. Are you sure you don't want a sweet roll?"

Sarah glanced back toward the tray that he had left sitting on a low stool. Then quick as a flash and hardly thinking, she struck the prince's hand. The silver goblet went flying, and the wine splashed on the wall.

"What are you doing?" the prince cried. "How dare you slap me!"

"Look, Prince!"

Alexander did look. Then, with a cry he ran and knelt beside the small golden-haired dog. "Shasta! What's wrong?"

Sarah stooped down by him and laid her hand on the dog. "She's dead, Prince Alex. I'm so sorry."

"How can she be dead?"

Sarah's mind was working quickly. "See? She ate some of the bread. And perhaps drank from the other goblet." She picked up the goblet and saw that it was nearly empty. "That's what it was," she whispered. "She drank this, and it had poison in it."

"Poison! How could that be?"

Gently, Sarah pulled him to his feet. "You're in danger here, Prince Alex. That poison was meant for you."

"I don't believe this!"

"You have to believe it. Your dog is dead."

The prince looked down with sorrow.

Sarah knew she had to take action. "We must get you out of here. You're at the mercy of . . . of anyone."

"But . . . but they guard my quarters. I can't go anywhere."

"Alex, you'd be dead if you had swallowed whatever was in that cup. Many people can get access here. Guards can be bribed. You're *not* safe. Someone wants to get you out of the way."

"You—perhaps you're right."

Sarah said, "I'll tell your father at once."

Sarah left the prince's rooms, but she did not go directly to the king. First, she sought out Josh and took him aside.

After Josh listened carefully to all she said, he nodded his head in agreement. "You're right, Sarah. We've got to get the prince out of here. He's the only hope of Madria. If he's dead, it's all over."

"Let's go to the king."

They went to the king's quarters but were told that he was too ill to see anyone.

"I know. Let's go to Dethenor," Sarah said. "He's the highest power under the king."

They found the old man in his office.

He took one look at their faces and admitted them at once. Then he listened while Sarah explained what had happened, and his own face turned pale.

"I knew it!" Dethenor whispered. "I knew it! We must do something quickly to save the prince's life."

"We think that the prince should be taken out of the palace and concealed where no one can get at him."

"I agree. But he's carefully watched. He can't leave his quarters . . ."

Josh smiled. "We'll find a way, Dethenor, with your permission. We've become pretty good at breaking out of jails."

"Very well," Dethenor said. "Do it. Tell no one what you're doing. We can trust nobody for a time."

"What about Alcindor?"

"Yes, you can trust him," Dethenor said instantly. "But no one else. Now, go quickly. There's not a moment to lose. If anything happens to the prince, the country will come under the authority of the Dark Lord, and I myself would rather die."

7
The Big Escape

Josh looked around the circle at the serious faces of his six friends. The thought passed through his mind, *We've done this before—quite a bit.*

He and Sarah had called them all for a quick war parley, and everyone had expressed shock at the attempt on Prince Alex's life—and Sarah's. Josh let them talk for a while, then broke into the hubbub of voices. "Wait a minute. We've got to make a plan, and I mean like now!"

"I'll tell you what I vote for," Reb said. "Let's buckle on our weapons and go charging in and get the prince out of there."

"That won't do," Dave said immediately. "There are guards on every floor. And even if we got out of the palace, we'd still have guards to contend with. And we don't know which ones are the enemy."

Reb argued valiantly that they could do it.

But Josh shook his head and said firmly, "Dave's right, Reb. We can't fight our way out of this one. Now, does anybody else have another idea?"

The talk went on for some time, and nothing workable seemed to come of it.

"Who do you think sent that poisoned food?" Abbey asked. "Whoever did that is the enemy."

"I know who it was," Wash said. "I've been watching that fellow Rondel, and he looks like a suspicious character to me."

"He looks suspicious to me too," Jake said. "He looks like the villain in an old gangster movie."

"It doesn't do any good to talk about who might have done this or that," Sarah said. "We've got to do something for the prince—and right away. Now, let's just be quiet for a moment and think."

The silence that fell over the room then seemed to stretch on and on. Occasionally someone would start to speak but then shake his head as if deciding some idea would not work.

All at once Jake sat straight up and slapped his hands together. "I know what! I've got it! I've got a master plan that'll work for sure!"

Reb looked at him with some doubt. "I've seen some of your master plans that didn't work too good," he said.

"Well, this one will work fine," Jake snapped. "See if it doesn't."

"So what is it, Jake?" Josh asked.

"It's real simple. The prince just walks out of his room, down the hall, down the stairs, across the courtyard, and out the palace gates."

"Oh, that's a wonderful plan!" Dave said sarcastically. "Only thing wrong with it is it won't work."

"No, wait, Dave. There's got to be more to your plan than that, Jake. Isn't there?" Josh asked. He studied the smaller boy, knowing that inside his skull was a keen brain, one that had often gotten them out of serious trouble.

"Now you listen to your Uncle Jake." He smirked. "I'll tell you how we're going to get Alex out of this. The first thing to understand is that people see what they want to see."

"What does that mean?" Wash demanded. "'People see what they want to see.'"

"Did you ever see a magician? Of course you have. What he does is get you to looking at his left hand. Then he does something with the right hand that you can't see because you're looking at his left hand."

"Stop talking in riddles," Josh growled. "What's the plan?"

"OK. Here it is. These big old chimneys take lots of cleaning, and they have chimney sweeps here just like they used to back in old England. I've seen them. You've all seen them around here—filthy and dirty, faces black."

"Sure, we've all seen them, Jake," Josh said impatiently. "What about it?"

"I figure this," Jake said slowly. "One of us that's about the same height as the prince gets into an outfit like that, black from head to foot, face all smeared, and he goes to clean the chimney in the prince's apartment."

Instantly Josh saw it. "I got you! When he gets in, he gives the prince his chimney-sweep clothes, and Alexander comes out and walks away, so dirty and black that the guards don't see any difference."

They talked about the plan for a while, and everybody liked it.

Josh said, "It's going to be difficult for the one who stays. He'll have to stay in the prince's quarters after Alex leaves, and when they find him they'll know he helped Alex make his escape."

"Well, it won't be either of you two girls," Dave said. "And it'll have to be Reb or me. We're the only two who are nearly as tall as the prince."

"I'll do it, Dave." Reb grinned. "And I know how I'll get out of there, too."

Reb would not reveal his plan for making an escape, but finally Josh said, "All right. That's what we'll do, then. Let's get at it."

The two guards standing outside the prince's apartment looked up as Sarah and her two companions approached. They had often seen the Sleepers and even knew their names. "Hello, Josh. Hello, Sarah," the guard Jent said. Then he grinned. "Who's that fine looking fellow with you?"

"He's come to clean the chimney," Josh said. "And we're going to visit the prince a little while."

His own mother would not have recognized Reb. He was clothed in the dirtiest possible, tattered clothing. His face was black, and he had a cap pulled down over his ears. It was also black. He grinned back at the guard. "Orders from the top. Clean the chimney in the prince's chambers, they said."

"Then go on in," Jent told them.

The three entered, and Alexander came toward them. "What in the world—"

Josh put a finger to his lips and held up his other hand in warning, as Sarah closed the door. "Be quiet," he whispered.

"What's going on here?" the prince whispered back. Then he looked at the sooty figure before him and said, "Who are you?"

"You know me all right, Prince," Reb said. "Just never saw me so dressed up before."

"Reb, is that *you?*"

"It's me."

"What's going on here?" the prince demanded.

"We talked to Dethenor," Sarah said quickly. "He agrees with us."

"What did my father say?"

"I'm afraid he was too ill for us to talk with him, but Dethenor says this is the wise thing to do."

"What is? And how am I going to get out of here?"

Reb laughed. "You're going to get out the way I came in. As a chimney sweeper."

The prince saw immediately what the plan was. But he began to argue. "I can't put myself in that kind of garb."

"It's better than being dead," Sarah said, "which is what you'll be if you stay here. Now what will it be?"

The prince flinched at her direct speech. "All right," he finally grumbled.

"Come on, Prince," Reb said. "You shuck out of those clothes and into these."

The boys changed clothes while Sarah turned her back. When Reb said, "OK," she turned around—and laughed.

Reb was a comical sight. His face was still black, although he had worn his own clothes underneath the rags. He went over to the wash basin, saying, "I'm going to wash this off. You put some of that soot on the prince, Sarah. Make sure he's as dirty as I was."

"Come on, Alex," Sarah said. "You've got to look just like Reb did."

It was not easy to persuade the prince. He was very fastidious, but Sarah insisted on smearing his face, his neck, and his hands with soot and even throwing more onto his filthy clothes. Then she frowned at his hair. "I really ought to cut that off," she said.

"You aren't going to cut my hair!"

"I think it'd be better, Prince Alex," Josh said.

"No! I'll put it under this cap. Nobody will see the difference."

The prince pushed his long hair under the floppy cap, and Josh and Sarah walked around him, looking him over.

"I guess he'll do," she decided.

"You'd better get on your way," Reb said. He was standing at the window.

"But what's your plan, Reb? How are you going to get out of here?" Sarah asked. "They might hang you for kidnapping the prince."

Reb reached down into the bag that held the tools he had brought for cleaning the chimney. "I got this and this." In one hand he held up a file and in the other a long rope. "I cut the bars with this and shinny down this rope. There won't be anything to it."

"Well, we're not leaving until the bars are cut," Josh said firmly.

They took turns filing through the two bars. Fortunately, the file was very keen. When they were filed through, the prince proved to be the strongest of them. He bent the cut bars upward so that there was room for Reb to squeeze through.

Reb grabbed the rope, tied it firmly to the bunk, and tossed the coil out the window. He looked out, then said, "You go on downstairs. I'll be behind the palace waiting for you when you come out."

"I guess we'd better go," Sarah said nervously.

The prince straightened up. "I feel like a fool in this outfit," he grumbled.

"You look fine. And we'll take the attention of the guards away from you. But don't say a word to anybody," Sarah warned.

"All right."

As they went out into the corridor, Sarah at once engaged the guards in conversation. "My, they must choose the best looking soldiers to be the guards to the prince!" she began with a smile.

The guards both grinned and did not pay one moment's attention to Josh and the blackened figure moving rapidly away from them and down the hall. As soon as Sarah saw them disappear around a corner, she said, "Well, you men do a great job. I hope you get your proper reward." She hurried after Josh and Alex, leaving the two guards grinning foolishly at each other.

As soon as Sarah caught up with them, Josh said, "I hope we get out of the palace as easily as we got out of Alex's quarters."

But all seemed to be going smoothly, just as Jake had said it would. *People are careful about those coming in,* Sarah thought, *but they don't pay much attention to those leaving.* Every guard merely gave them a nod, and they walked out of the palace.

"I just hope Reb is down safely," Josh said. "I'd break my neck if I tried to slide down a rope like that."

They turned immediately to their right, hurrying along in the falling darkness. As they turned the corner to the back of the palace, a voice said, "Well, you took your time. I've been waiting here for a week."

"Reb! You made it all right!"

"Slicker than goose grease," Reb said cheerfully. He looked up at the rope still dangling from the window. "Easier coming down than it would be going up."

"We'd better get moving," Josh said.

They hurried to the stables, where they found the other Sleepers ready and waiting.

"Did you get a good horse for the prince?"

"I want my own horse," Prince Alex said.

"Not a chance," Sarah said quickly. "It would be recognized right away. What you need is a good, solid homely horse with no attractiveness whatsoever."

"Just the one I've got." Dave patted the rump of a mousy brown animal. It looked strong but certainly not flashy.

"Quick, then. Everybody mount. We've got to get away from here," Josh urged.

They swung into the saddles and rode out. The gates were opened for them without a question, and they passed out of the palace grounds and thundered down the road. Josh led the way at a full gallop, wanting to put as much distance as he could between the prince and the palace.

"Where are we going?" Sarah asked him.

"To a place called the Deep Forest. It's a place Dethenor told me about it. Hardly anybody goes there, he says. People think it's haunted."

"Good," Sarah said. She was leaning over her horse's neck. When she looked back, she could see the prince riding bolt upright. The moon was coming up, and she could even see the soot on his face. "We've got the prince out, but what good does it do us in the long run?"

"Don't know. At least we've got time now."

Sarah kept even with Josh, and the others followed closely. Finally she said, "And it gives us time to work on Prince Alexander. He's got to learn the hard way how life is—just like us ordinary mortals do."

8

The Prince and
the Firewood

Josh came out of a sound sleep very slowly. He was aware that his body was sore all over, and he rolled over and snorted and tried to go back to sleep. Then a bird began singing close by, and opening his eyes to a slant, he saw that dawn had arrived.

With a groan he sat up and looked around. The other Sleepers and the prince were all lumps in the gray darkness, wrapped in their blankets against the cold of the night. He staggered to his feet and stretched his aching muscles.

"That was a hard ride and a hard piece of ground," he muttered. "But at least we're away from the palace."

The bird began singing a louder song now, and Josh grumbled, "What have you got to be so cheerful about so early?" He'd grown rather expert at telling time without a watch since coming to NuWorld, and now he estimated that it was almost six o'clock. He walked over to where Wash was sleeping and poked him with his socked foot. "Get up, Wash," he said. "It's past sunrise." Moving on, he did the same with Dave and was greeted with a hoarse voice saying, "Get away and leave me alone!"

Josh grinned, went back, and pulled on his boots. They had all slept in their clothes and hadn't eaten supper. They'd been too weary to cook a meal after riding half the night.

He walked down to the stream and washed his face in its cold water, snorting and shivering. He ran his hands through his hair, then turned back to the camp, where he found everyone more or less awake. The girls had found a private spot to sleep, and as they rejoined the boys, Abbey was complaining as usual about her looks.

"I'm a mess!" she said. "I've got to wash my hair."

"Wash all you want to, but the first order of business is to get something to eat."

"That's a good idea," Jake said. "My stomach thinks my throat's been cut."

The prince was standing off by himself. They had paused long enough last night for him to wash the soot off his face and to clothe himself in an outfit that was very unprincelike but clean. It was a simple costume of rough brown material consisting of britches and a tunic. The shoes were made of leather but were old and cracked.

Recalling what Sarah had said about teaching the prince something about humility, Josh had an idea.

"We'll divide up the work. Wash, you cook the breakfast this morning. Prince Alex, you go cut the firewood."

As Josh had expected, Alexander straightened up, and his face flushed. "A prince," he announced firmly, "does not cut firewood!"

Josh saw that the others were all watching. They were well aware of the prince's arrogance, and Josh knew that it was time to set the lines of battle. "Prince," he said, "you may not cut firewood. But if you don't, you won't eat."

"I don't care anything about that! You don't have anything fit to eat anyway!"

Josh said, "You may feel differently after another hard day's travel. We probably won't stop to eat at noon, so you won't have anything until tonight. And even then you won't eat if you won't cut firewood."

"I do not take orders from you," Prince Alex said loftily. He stalked down to the stream, where he knelt for a drink.

"What are you going to do with him, Josh?" Sarah murmured.

"Let him go hungry. When he's hungry enough, he'll cut firewood."

"It must be hard for him," she mused. "He's had everything done for him all of his life, and now he doesn't have any servants. Taking orders from somebody younger—it must be really galling to him."

"He's got to learn," Josh said grimly. "Now let's get busy."

The wood was gathered, though not by Alex, and the breakfast got cooked. The smell of frying bacon was in the air. Josh, who had helped Wash by frying it, looked up and called, "Come and get it!"

Everyone came at once to gather around. Josh put bacon slices on their tin plates, and Wash added fried potatoes. Sarah sliced some bread. All in all, it was a pretty good meal. They ate as though half-starved, and as Jake wolfed down his breakfast, he nodded toward the prince standing at a distance, trying to look disinterested.

"I bet he's hungry as a wolf," he mumbled to Abbey. "And all he had to do was cut a little firewood."

"You've never been a prince, Jake," Abbey said. "You don't know what that's like."

"I know what it's like to be hungry, though, and I'd rather cut firewood than be hungry—even if I *was* a prince." He swallowed another bite of bacon and glanced over at Josh. "Are you going to hold out, Josh, and let him go hungry?"

"It's his own choice," Josh said. He did not like what was happening, but he knew that part of the prince's education would have to be learning to work together with others. Alexander seemingly had never done that in his whole life, and Josh knew it would be hard.

After breakfast, he called, "Prince Alex, if you wash the dishes, you can have the leftovers."

Alexander gave him a hard look. Then he turned and walked to his horse and began to saddle it.

"I'm worried about him, Josh," Sarah whispered.

"Well, don't worry. He won't starve. He's got to come down from that ivory tower sooner or later."

Traveling proved to be very difficult. The Deep Forest was still almost a day's journey away, and they had to keep off the main roads. The horses grew weary, and so did their riders. Josh did let everybody stop at noon, but only long enough to allow them to eat a little of the leftover bacon from breakfast. He pointedly did not offer any to the prince.

They reached the edge of the Deep Forest late in the day, just as the sun was starting down over the hills. They unsaddled their horses, and Josh said in the hearing of everyone, "Well, Prince, are you going to join us and do a little of the work?"

"No!"

"Very well. It's your choice. You may be a little overweight, but you won't be if you keep this up."

The others, accustomed to working together, quickly made a camp and cooked what was left of the meat. Once again the frying bacon made a sizzling noise, and the odor was irresistible. Reb had gone off and caught some small fish, and the frying fish smelled good, too.

Prince Alex sat by himself while the others ate and laughed and talked. Josh was sure that the prince was miserable but would not admit it. No doubt he felt lonely and left out. Besides, he would know that the Sleepers had risked their lives for him. In fact, Josh decided, Alex was likely ready to give up and do whatever they asked, but his pride kept him from it.

After they had eaten supper, the little group sat around the campfire. It was a rather cheerful time. The fire made a pleasant crackling sound, and from time to time one of them would poke at the burning logs, sending showers of fiery sparks upward to mingle with the stars. Or so it seemed. The evening was cool, and all but Alexander hugged the fire and drew their blankets around them.

Reb began telling stories of his hunting days back in Arkansas in OldWorld. He was a natural-born storyteller and soon had them all hanging onto his words, sometimes laughing and sometimes commenting on the excitement of those days.

Sarah did not join in very often. She sat back from the fire just a little, and her glance went to Prince Alex. He was sitting with his back to a tree and a blanket around him. His head drooped, so that she could not see his face. But she could imagine he was lonely. *It's a shame*, she thought. *It's a shame that he has to learn in such a hard way. But he's got to learn how other people feel, and he's got to learn that he can't always have his own way. Not even a king can do that.*

71

At last Josh said, "Better turn in. We'll have a busy day tomorrow."

Soon they were rolled in their blankets and quiet, but for a long time Sarah lay awake, watching the glow of the fire. When she finally did doze off, she was abruptly awakened by a loud noise and a yell almost by her head. She came out of her blanket, grasping for a weapon.

"What's going on here?" Josh demanded.

Reb was standing next to the prince and holding onto his right arm. "Why, we've got us a grub thief here. The prince of Madria was stealing food!"

"Turn me loose," Alexander said, and he tried to free himself from Reb's grasp.

"You know it's not good to steal from your friends," Reb said.

The remark infuriated the prince. He turned and drove a blow at Reb's head.

Reb was younger but faster. He caught Alex's fist and flipped the prince over his shoulder. Alexander struck the ground hard, and Sarah heard a *whoof* as his breath was expelled.

"Let him alone, Reb. That's enough," Josh said. As the prince struggled to his feet, Josh helped him. "I'm sorry this happened, Prince Alex."

Prince Alexander stood as humiliated as surely he had ever been. "I'll leave," he said. "You don't want me here."

"You mustn't do that, Prince," Josh said.

"You don't want me here."

"We do want you here. We've gone to great trouble to get you here. The only thing is that you've been brought up in a different way, and now it's time for you to learn that there are other people to consider besides yourself."

This time Prince Alex took Josh's lecture without saying another word.

"I think you've said enough, Josh," Sarah said quietly. "Prince Alex, please try not to be too discouraged. I know your world's fallen down, but we're really your friends, and we want to help you. Won't you just join us and let us be your friends?"

Maybe Prince Alex finally realized that he had been refusing to do a simple bit of work for people who were risking their lives for him. In any case, he straightened up, looked straight at Josh, and said, "It's all right. I'll chop the firewood and do anything else that you order."

"Why, that's wonderful, Prince. And I think you deserve something to eat. Let's all have a midnight snack."

While the prince watched, the Sleepers scurried around to find some food. Sarah gave him a piece of good, leftover fish, and Jake urged on him a piece of bacon that he had been saving. The talk was cheerful.

Then Alex abruptly turned to Sarah. "You were right," he said. "I've been a spoiled brat."

"It's not altogether your fault," she said gently. "It must be hard for anyone who has everything to learn how to live with others. But, Alex, you know that most of the subjects in your country are poor people. How can you govern them if you don't know anything about them? You've got to learn to understand them and what they need, and I think this is a good opportunity. Don't you?"

The prince said quietly, "I don't know if I can learn, Sarah."

Impulsively she put her hand on his arm. "Yes, you can, and we'll help you."

"You will?"

"Yes. That's what we came for." She smiled and said, "Now, let's all go to sleep, and tomorrow will be a new day."

Rondel was in a rage. He looked as if he wanted to put his hands around Count Ferrod's throat and choke him. "You let the prince *escape?*"

"It's not our fault!" the countess cried. "I tried to do away with him as you said, but somehow he avoided the trap."

"And I know how. The Seven Sleepers," Rondel said.

The count tried to calm him down. "We'll find him," he said quietly. "I have men out searching."

"Well, you've been fools, but all is not lost."

"What are you thinking, Rondel?" the countess asked.

"The prince may have escaped our trap, but he will never be king of Madria."

"Why do you say that?"

"Because the weapon that the Zorians have been waiting for is almost ready."

"What is this weapon?" Ferrod asked. "Is it a new kind of bow?"

"Something much better than that. You will find out when it comes—which will not be long."

"So our country will be taken over by the Zorians?"

"The king will have to abdicate—he's too ill to serve, anyway. With some . . . guidance . . . the Council will choose a new ruler. And we know who that ruler will be, don't we?"

Count Ferrod understood, but rather than feeling happy, he felt he had been drawn into a trap and there was no way out. He did not like what was happening. He said hopefully, "The prince is gone. There will be no need to hunt him down and kill him."

"A prince is always a danger to a man like yourself. He must die, and the Sleepers and Dethenor must die with him."

9

The Training of a Soldier

Josh and his friends were so well hidden from the busy, inhabited parts of the kingdom that they had ceased to be fearful of discovery. They were aware of patrols that came out from time to time, but the Sleepers had their own guard system. When an alert was sounded, they quickly retreated to a deeper part of the woods. They spent most of their time getting ready for the battle to come. Josh, especially, wanted to see the prince develop into a first-class soldier.

"We'll have to be like top sergeants back in the old days," he told Reb. "You don't make good soldiers by sitting down and eating ice cream sundaes."

"You mean," Reb said, "you want me to pour it on him."

"That's right. He's got to learn to fight, he's got to learn to endure hardships, and I'm putting you in charge of seeing that it gets done."

Reb went at the business of training the prince with a vengeance. He rousted him out before daylight every morning and took him on hard treks through the deep woods and up and down the mountainside. He completely ignored Alexander's protests.

One Thursday morning, Sarah was up early enough to talk with Reb about the prince's progress. "How is he doing, Reb?"

"He's not doing bad at all," Reb admitted. "He's strong and quick, and when he gets in shape, he'll be a first-rate soldier. All that easy living has made him soft, but I'll take care of that."

"Don't be too hard on him, Reb," she warned. "You don't want to get him out of the notion of serving."

"Don't worry. He'll be as good as one of Stonewall Jackson's boys." It was the highest praise he could give.

He roughly roused the prince by shaking his shoulder. "Get up, Prince. Time to go to work."

Alex came out of a deep sleep and sat up. If his muscles ached from yesterday's longer-than-usual hike up steep mountain trails, he refused to show it. "Then let's get at it," he said cheerfully.

"That's the way to talk. Come along. We'll cook us breakfast and be on our way."

They did their cooking in the semidarkness, and Alexander ate heartily. Reb noticed that the prince washed his own plate, and he thought, *He wouldn't have done that before. We're getting somewhere.*

"We'll take some sword practice before we do anything else," Reb told him.

They picked up their weapons, and Reb led Alex far out from the camp where the noise would not awaken the others. "All right," he said, turning to face the prince, "let's see what you got."

Alexander advanced. These were broadswords, not fencing foils, and it took a strong arm to wield them. The prince was the stronger of the two and Reb the quicker. Time and time again, Alexander would shower blows down, but Reb quickly parried them. Several times Reb could have touched the prince, but he did not. Finally, however, Reb called out, "That's enough! I'm out of breath."

The prince was breathing hard, too, but he seemed

pleased with the exercise. "This is a lot of fun, Reb. It never was before."

"It's fun, but it's more than that," Reb said. "When a battle starts and you cross swords with someone, which one of you wins probably will be the one that's practiced the most." He rested against a tree and broke off a weed. He held the stem between his teeth and nodded approvingly. "Practice makes perfect," he said. "You've come a long way."

Alex looked pleased at the praise. They stood talking until Reb said, "Now let's do some fast walking today."

They hiked along, carrying nothing but their weapons, and Reb was pleased that Alex was able to keep up with him. He had not been able to do that at first, but now he matched him step for step.

"What was it like back in your world? What you call OldWorld, Reb."

"What was it like? Well, it was a lot different from this."

"Who ruled your world?"

"Well, nobody ruled the *world*. Every country had its own king or its own president."

"Did your country have a king?"

"For a while. Then we fought a war to get rid of our king."

Alex stared at him with surprise. "You were traitors?"

Reb shook his head. "No, no. You don't understand. Let me try to give you a quick history lesson. It was because our people thought they were not treated fairly, and they tried everything they could to get fair treatment. Finally, when they couldn't, they declared their independence. It was called the American Revolution."

"Then who ruled after you got your independence?"

Reb broke into a trot. "Let's speed it up." He tried to think of the best way to explain. "They had elections back in OldWorld America. People would vote, and the man that got the most votes was the president."

"So who voted?"

"Well, just the men at first, but after a while the women too."

As they flew swiftly along the trail, the prince kept asking questions. When they stopped for a break and a drink of water at a small brook, he said, "I don't see how it would work. What if the wrong man was elected?"

"Sometimes that happened," Reb said, "but sometimes the wrong man gets to be king. Isn't that right?"

"I guess so. Still, I don't think our people would want a president. They like a king."

After the two hiked all morning, Reb said, "Time to go back, but I'm sure hungry."

"Too bad we didn't bring along something to eat."

"I'll tell you what. Let's catch a fish out of this stream. We could start a fire, skin him, and have fish for lunch."

"We didn't bring any hooks or . . ."

Reb laughed. "I'll show you how to get a fish without a hook. It's called *noodling*."

"Noodling?" The prince's brow furrowed. "What's noodling?"

"I'll show you." Reb walked slowly along the brook until he found a spot he liked. "You see that log over there? I just saw something move in the water beside it."

The prince looked at the old log lying half underwater. He watched a moment, then nodded. "Something's in there, all right."

"Probably a big catfish. You just stay and watch your Uncle Reb do his stuff."

"Could I help you?"

"If you want to," Reb said. "Not everybody likes it. Some people are afraid to do it."

"I'm not afraid," Prince Alex said quickly.

"OK. Come on."

Reb stepped into the water, and they waded out to the log, where the water was waist deep. He said, "Now we're going to be real still, and what you do is you put your hand under this log."

"What if there's a snake under there?"

Reb grinned. "You'd probably get bit, but they don't stay underwater much. Of course, a big turtle might be under there. I never got bit by one. It's always possible, though."

The prince placed his hand under the log, and Reb said, "Now you just feel along it, moving real slow. If we have any luck, we'll find a big catfish lying under there. In the heat of the day is the best time to catch him—like right now."

The prince probably did not like putting his hand under the log, but he did as Reb said. Finally he exclaimed softly, "I touched something! It was soft, and it moved."

"That's it!" Reb said excitedly. "Now here's what you do next. Slip your hand under the fish's belly and stroke it."

"Stroke his belly?"

"That's it. That makes them go to sleep—I think."

The prince did as he was instructed, and Reb grinned. He had not expected the king's son to show so much nerve.

"Now you be careful of his spines. They've got poison in them. Don't get involved with them. What you do is slip your right hand up, put your thumb in his mouth, and then with one motion you clamp down and you lift him up and you throw him to the bank."

Apprehensively, the prince followed his instructions. "I've got up to his mouth," he said. "He's a big fish."

"You have to do it smoothly now. Grab him and throw!"

The prince may have fully expected to be bitten or stabbed with one of the spines, but he appeared to clamp his hand down on the fish's jaw. Then with one motion he flung onto the bank a catfish that weighed close to four or five pounds.

"You got him, Alex! You got him!" Reb scrambled to the bank and stopped the fish's flopping with his boot.

The prince waded out and stared at the fish. "I never thought I could do a thing like that."

"So now we can have lunch," Reb said. "You cut us some sticks to put the meat on, and I'll dress this fellow out."

"Let me clean him," Prince Alex said. "I've never cleaned a fish before."

"OK, but it's a messy job."

The prince gave Reb a direct look. "I'm going to have to take over some messy jobs," he said. Then he listened to Reb's instructions and followed them carefully. When it was over, his hands were messy indeed, but he was grinning. "And now I know how to noodle."

"You learn quick, Alex. When you set your mind on a job, you do it. Well, let's have lunch."

The day after the prince noodled his fish, Alcindor arrived. He had come before both to bring them news and to see how the prince was doing, but this time there was a worried look on his face.

Everyone gathered about him.

Alcindor stared at Alex. "Good morning, my Prince."

"Good morning, Alcindor."

"You're sunburned."

"Yes, I suppose I am," the prince said simply.

Then the aide said, "Well, I wish I were the bearer of good tidings, but I'm not."

"What's happening, Alcindor?" Alexander asked quickly.

"The pressure is building up. There will certainly be a Zorian attack very soon. Their troops are moving to the front lines right on the other side of the mountains. Something's going to happen. And more than that, the Madrian patrols are thick, looking for *you*. The king and queen are worried about you."

"You tell them that I am doing fine. Tell them I'm learning to be a soldier."

Alcindor smiled suddenly. "That's got to be good news for them." Then he added, "But you can't stay in this place any longer. The patrols are moving this way."

"Where can we go?" Josh asked. "Farther back in the woods?"

"No. They will surely find you there," Alcindor said. "I suggest you go to a village called Pellenor. Find a family there called Starbuck. Starbuck is a good man. He's been loyal to the king always."

"Shall I tell him who I am?" the prince asked.

"No. Better to keep it a secret. Indeed, disguise yourself the best you can while there. Even act mentally unbalanced, if you have to."

They made their plans, and Alcindor suggested

something else. "I don't think all of you should go to the Starbuck farm, either. The rest of you disperse but have a central meeting point. Stay there until the time comes."

"What time?" the prince asked quickly.

Alcindor drew up straight and tall, and he smiled faintly. "Until the time we must all put our lives at risk." A cloud came into his fine gray eyes, and he shook his head. "I do not think it will be long."

10
A New Line of Work

The sun was dropping behind the distant hills as Sarah and Prince Alex approached the farmhouse. Some stars were already visible, and Sarah said with some apprehension, "This looks like the place that Alcindor described as the Starbuck farm. But I wish we could have gotten here before dark."

Alexander peered ahead into the gathering darkness. "We have no other choice," he said. "Unless we want to sleep out in the woods and go in early in the morning."

"No, let's go in now. And remember, Alex. Remember you're *not* a prince. You have to have another name." She thought and said, "It should be a name that sounds something like Alex. So let's just say your name is Lex."

"If you say so," the prince agreed.

They neared the main farmhouse, and Sarah called out, "Hello, the house!"

Almost at once a man emerged. He was bent over and walking with the help of a cane. "Hello," he said. "It's late for travelers to be out."

"We're looking for the Starbuck farm."

"You've found it. I'm Joss Starbuck." He was not a large man, and as Sarah drew closer to examine his face, she saw that he had the marks of pain that an invalid sometimes has. Lowering her voice, although no one was near, she said, "Alcindor sent us."

This apparently surprised Joss Starbuck but did not alarm him. "Alcindor has been a good friend to me. Won't you come inside?"

The two followed the farmer into the house, which was neat and well kept. Starbuck turned to them then, and his eyes narrowed. "I expect you want a favor. People who come from Alcindor usually do."

"We need to hide out here for a while, sir. My name is Sarah, and this is Lex."

She expected the farmer to ask questions, but he merely looked them over, then nodded. "If Alcindor says it's all right, it must be. I assume you want to work in order to look like part of the hired help."

"Yes," Sarah said quickly. "That would be fine."

"Well, you can help with the housework, Sarah. And, Lex, you can work in the fields."

Sarah quickly answered for the prince. "That will be fine, too."

"The young lady can room in the house. And there's a bunkhouse for you outside, Lex. Our hired men left, so actually we *need* help pretty badly."

The farmer showed Sarah to her quarters. She saw she would be staying in a very neat room with a large window looking out over the spacious countryside. She was grateful.

Joss Starbuck took Alex to a building behind the barn. It had two sets of bunk beds and a washstand—and a stove. But he said, "You can eat with us in the big house."

"How many people help you on the farm?"

"Ordinarily four, but they took off and left us. Scared of the war that's coming."

Alex looked at the older man curiously. "How do they know war is coming?"

"How do they know!" Starbuck exclaimed. "Everybody knows the Zorians are massing over on the other side of the mountains. They're not coming to have a tea party."

"Then we'll just have to stop them," Alex said grimly.

"That sounds like Alcindor." But the farmer looked pleased. "We'll wake you up early in the morning. There's a lot of work to be done. You may be hiding from somebody, but we can use your help." He turned and left.

Alexander washed his face and flopped on a bunk without even undressing. He slept a dreamless sleep.

Suddenly, somebody was pounding at Alex's door. Next, a voice was yelling, "Get up! Get out of that bed! You can't sleep all day. Come on. What's your name?"

Alex sat straight up in the bunk and looked wildly around. Now he saw that a young woman had pushed open the door! "Who are *you?*" he demanded.

She was tall and athletic looking. She had blonde hair and green eyes. She was wearing a light blue tunic. And she did not look friendly.

The girl put her hands on her hips and said, "What are you staring at? I'm Lilith Starbuck. My father tells me you're here to work, so let's get at it."

"All right," Alex said. He stood up and said, "Do we get to eat before we work?"

"Breakfast is ready in the big house." Then she left.

Alex washed his face at the washstand, still puzzling over this bossy girl. He splashed himself liberally, ran his hands through his thick, auburn hair, then went around to the main house. There he found the table set, and Sarah, wearing an apron, was placing dishes on the table.

"Sit down, Lex," Joss said. "I believe Sarah here has made one of the best breakfasts I've ever seen. If it tastes as good as it looks, it's all right."

The four of them sat down to the breakfast that Sarah had prepared, which included ham and eggs and fresh breads. Prince Alex ate hungrily, for neither he nor Sarah had had supper last night.

Lilith cocked her head to one side. "If you can work as well as you can eat, you'll be of some help around here."

Sarah smiled at that. She said, "What's to be done today?"

"Quite a bit. We've got to weed out the corn, and that will be a big job," the girl said.

Before long, Joss and Lilith began talking about conditions in the kingdom. Joss Starbuck put a bad face on it, but it was Lilith who snapped, "If the king's son were worth a copper coin, we might have a chance! But all he wants to do is party and have fun!"

"Perhaps you shouldn't talk about people you don't know!" Alex said sharply.

Lilith turned her eyes to him with surprise. "Don't tell me you stand up for that no-good prince!"

Sarah put in quickly, "I'm sure Prince Alexander has some good features."

"He has good features all right. He knows how to play and ignore all of his duties. I'd like to have him here. I'd tell him a thing or two."

"He might spank you," Alex said. He hoped he was covering his anger. "I hear the prince doesn't like impudent women."

"I'd like to see him try it!" Lilith had a table knife in her hand, and she gestured with it. "But no danger of that. He's too busy enjoying himself to come and do anything as low as working on a farm."

Sarah managed to change the subject. After they had finished eating, she said, "I'll be working in the house today, Lex."

"And he'll be outside helping me," Lilith said. "Although I don't think he can keep up with a real worker."

"Like you?" Alex asked.

"That's right! You've probably never done a day's work in your life. We've had your kind here before. I'll work him until he falls, Father," she said. "Well, come on. It's time to get to work." She got up and strode out of the kitchen.

Alexander followed her.

"She means well," Lilith's father said apologetically to Sarah. "But she may be a little rough sometimes. She hasn't had much fine raising."

"She's a nice girl and beautiful. I know you're very proud of her."

"We lost her mother five years ago. She's been very lonesome since then," Joss said thoughtfully. "But she takes care of me, does all the housework and all the cooking. I *am* proud of her."

"She was a little hard on the prince."

"Yes, she was, but then everybody in the kingdom knows the prince isn't the man his father was."

"Maybe he'll change."

"I hope so," Joss said, wagging his head sadly. "It's a shame for a young man with all his opportunities to waste them."

Lilith led Alex out to a very large field. She handed him a hoe and said, "Now, you know how to hoe corn?"

"No, I don't."

Grabbing the hoe from him, Lilith made a few quick strokes and cut the grass that had grown between two stalks of corn. "This may be too difficult for you to understand, but you have to chop the weeds just like this. You think you can remember that?"

He glared at her. "I can remember. Give me that hoe."

Alex began to work, and soon the sun overhead brought a fine sweat to his face. The hoe was too short for him, and he had to lean over. So his back began to hurt. Up one long row he went, then back another. He looked up occasionally to see Lilith doing the same sort of work farther down in the field.

He had been at the job for about two hours when she suddenly appeared with a jug of water. "Here. Drink this."

Quickly Alex dropped the hoe and seized the jug. He let the delicious, cool water slide down his dry throat. Finally he was satisfied, and he handed the jug back. "Thanks," he said.

"You're welcome." She looked down the row he had hoed and said, "You're missing some grass. Be more careful." Without another word she walked away.

Alex said under his breath, "Impudent girl! She does need a spanking."

The morning wore on slowly. By the time the sun was directly overhead, Alex could hardly stand up. He sat down in the row to rest and pulled his broad hat down over his face. Suddenly he was very tired. He went to sleep sitting there.

He was awakened some time later when something struck him on the shoulder. He jumped up to see that Lilith had been tapping him with her hoe handle.

"You will never touch me again!" he cried crossly. "You understand that?"

Lilith ignored that and glared up at him. It was obvious she thought he was not much of a worker. "You can't even work for a whole day!" she taunted. "What makes you so special?"

"I can accomplish any work I choose to," he said.

"Can you? Then we'll see. We'll go to the house to eat, and then we'll see who can chop the most rows this afternoon. My wager is that the woman will be the victor."

Something about the girl's independence pleased Alex, but at the same time he wondered if she ever had a more womanly side.

Back at the house, they ate a good midday meal—prepared by Sarah—and Alex drank plenty of cool water. He hoped Lilith would give them an hour's rest.

But as soon as she finished eating, Lilith said, "All right. Let's go back." And she winked at Sarah. "We have a contest going to see who can hoe the most corn."

Her father shook his head. "Don't let her work you to death, Lex. She loves work the way other girls like pretty clothes."

Getting through the afternoon was difficult, but by working as fast as he could, Alex managed to hoe as many rows as Lilith did. When the sun was low in the sky, she came by and looked at his work. "That's a good job," she said with some surprise. "I didn't think you could do it."

Alex did not say a word. His back was aching, and his palms were covered with blisters. Some of them had even bled.

"Enough for today. Let's go in and have supper," Lilith said.

The supper was good. Sarah had outdone herself again, but Alex was so tired, and his back ached, and his hands hurt so badly he could not join in the conversation. When he had finished eating, he said, "I think I'll go to bed early."

"We'll get in another good day's work tomorrow. See if you can hold up, Lex." Lilith smiled.

After the prince had left for the bunkhouse, Sarah said, "As you see, he's willing to work, Lilith, but he's not used to this *kind* of work."

"No, I saw that right away," Lilith said. Then she eyed Sarah curiously. "What are you two doing here anyway? Father tells me you're hiding from something."

Alarmed, Sarah said, "You must never say anything like that publicly, Lilith! If we are found, it would be very bad."

"But Alcindor sent you," Lilith said thoughtfully. "So you must be all right."

Alex went to an outside shower, where he washed off some of the sweat and the dirt. The water felt good, indeed. He went back to his room and lay down on the bunk, exhausted. His hands hurt.

The door swung open almost at once, and Lilith marched in with a basin of water and some other things on a tray.

"Do you know how to knock?" Alex demanded grumpily.

She put down the tray and said, "Sit up."

Alex sat up, wondering what she was doing.

"Let me see your hands."

Alex extended his hands, palms down.

92

She turned them over and took a deep breath. "I thought so. You should have told me that you were getting blisters. I would have gotten you some gloves."

"You didn't ask."

Lilith looked at him and frowned. "Your hands are pitiful. I've brought some salve that will make them feel better."

She rinsed and dried his hands, then opened a small jar and began to put the salve on his palms. "I know this is painful," she said. "We'll find some work for you tomorrow that won't be as hard."

"Thank you. That feels better," Alex said when she finished. "I'm sure I can do more hoeing tomorrow."

"There's other work that's not as hard on the hands. Can you milk a cow?"

"No."

"Maybe I'll teach you how to do that." She sat for a few moments then, looking at him curiously. "What have you been doing with yourself?"

Prince Alexander knew she meant the question to be innocent enough, but it somehow hit him hard. He thought of how wasteful he had been of all the gifts that he had and how he had thrown away his opportunities.

"Nothing to be proud of," he said, looking away.

Lilith seemed surprised at this answer. But she said, "Well, Lex, you're still young. You can make anything you want to of yourself."

"Like a farmer?"

"Of course. You're strong, and that's important. Would you like to be a farmer?"

"Lilith, I don't know what I want to be. Except I don't want to be what I have been." He looked at her oddly and then smiled. "What about you?" He had never talked much to a commoner and was suddenly very curious. "What will you do?"

"What will I do?" Lilith said with surprise. "I'll work. I'll marry. I'll have children. I'll help people all I can. That's what I'll do."

"That sounds like a good thing," the prince said. "You do that, Lilith."

She rose to her feet and went to the door, where she turned back and smiled a warm smile. "Tomorrow morning—if your hands are well enough—I'll teach you how to milk a cow. Then we can gather some eggs. And then maybe we'll do something fun instead of just work."

"All right, Lilith," he said. "If that's what you want, I'll do it. Good night."

"Good night, Lex."

And he knew that she had lost her dislike for him.

11
The Wager

B elieve it or not, Josh, Prince Alex is doing much better."

Sarah had gone to the spot where she and Josh agreed to meet each day. It was not difficult for her to get away from the farm, for Joss Starbuck was not a harsh taskmaster. Besides, he always lay down for a rest in the afternoon. Now they stood beside the road under a large spreading tree.

"Well, that's good to hear," Josh said. But he studied her face. Then he asked seriously, "Sarah, do you *really* think there's a chance that he could be changing?"

"I do think so," she assured him, and a smile came to her lips. "In fact, he's learning to milk a cow. I don't think the old Prince Alex would have stooped to such a thing as that."

"Milk a cow!"

"Lilith is teaching him how. As I told you, she didn't care for him much at first, but now I think she's accepted him."

"And you're sure that no one knows you're here? Or at least doesn't know who you are."

"I think we're all right so far. Joss Starbuck works outside all day, so no one comes to the house to see him. And there's very little traffic along the road. Patrols do come by once in a while. One of them stopped the day before yesterday, I think it was, for water at the well. They asked Joss if any strangers had been around, and he told them no, there weren't. Just his workers."

"Well, that's good." Josh breathed a sigh of relief. "For I think it's pretty clear that the prince's enemies are going to stop at nothing."

"How are things going back in the capital, Josh? Have you talked to Alcindor lately?"

"Yes." A furrow creased his brow. "The news is not good, I'm afraid. Reports keep coming in about some awful weapon that the Zorians have developed."

"Does anyone have any idea at all what it is?"

"No one can figure it out," Josh said. "We know it must have something to do with getting through the passes, but how they would do that—and with what kind of a weapon—no one seems to know."

"I do hope nothing happens for a while. It takes time to transform a worthless son into a real prince."

When Alex finished hoeing his last row of corn, he walked along to where Lilith was close to the end of her own final row. He waited until she finished. When she stopped hoeing and looked up at him with a question in her eyes, he asked, "Don't you ever do anything but work?"

"Of course I do. I do a lot of things."

"Like what?"

"Why are you so curious about me, Lex?"

"I'm just interested. Come now. Tell me. What do you do when you're not working? Work is all I've ever seen you do."

"Well, I go to the village and look in the shops. I go on picnics with my friends. Sometimes there are parties and folk dances when all the farmers get together with their families. Sometimes I go fishing."

"There's an idea!" Alex glanced up at the sky. "We've got a couple hours of daylight left. Do you fish close by?"

"Oh yes. The river's right over there."

"Then let's go."

Lilith laughed. "You've certainly come a long way. At first you couldn't last a day of work, and now you're working all day and still having enough energy left to go fishing."

"Guess I'm becoming a farmer." The thought amused him, and he grinned. He also suspected that Lilith prided herself on being a good fisherman. "I'll bet I catch more fish than you do."

"We'll see about that. Come on, then. We'll get the poles, and we'll see who's the best fisherman."

Twenty minutes later, they were approaching the river. It was only about thirty feet across, but it was a beautiful stream, running over rocks and making a melodious gurgling sound. Big trees hung over it from both sides. When they reached the water, Alex said, "This would be a good place to go swimming."

"I do that, too, sometimes. There's a deep place for swimming about a quarter of a mile down, but the best fishing is right here."

They baited their hooks and began slowly moving along the stream. For a time they caught only small fish, not big enough to keep.

They stopped where the river made a bend and a big tree had fallen. "Let's sit here and wait them out. Perhaps if we are still—and patient—we'll get some fish," Lilith said.

"Suits me."

They sat down on the log and for a time were silent. When a deer appeared downstream, they sat very still. He came cautiously toward them, a fine ten-point buck. He stooped to drink, then suddenly realized that they were watching him. Snorting, he sprang away with long, lovely leaps and disappeared into the trees.

"Isn't it beautiful the way those deer can run and jump?" Lilith said. "I think they're the most beautiful creatures in the world."

"Oh, I've seen things more beautiful than that." And Alex smiled at her.

They spent perhaps an hour on the log, fishing and talking and asking questions about each other's lives. Alex found it rather difficult to keep Lilith satisfied, for he could not reveal his true identity. Finally, he looked up at the sky and said, "Well, it's almost dark, and we didn't catch any fish after all."

"I can't understand why they're not biting," she said.

A thought came to Alex then, and he said, "Remember the wager we made about who could catch the most fish?"

"Of course."

"How about another little wager?"

"I really don't like wagers," Lilith said. But clearly she was curious. "What kind of wager are you talking about this time?"

"I'll wager that I can catch a fish big enough to feed all of us. Your father and Sarah included."

"You can't!"

"You want to wager?"

Lilith said, "I've fished in this river all my life. When the fish aren't biting—they simply aren't biting. But, all right. What shall we wager?"

"Oh, something fun."

"Something like what?"

"Well . . ." He thought. "How about . . . if I catch a fish big enough to feed us all, you have to call me 'Sir Lex'? And curtsy before me just as if I were a prince. And you have to wait on me at the supper table. In short, treat me like royalty for the rest of the day."

Lilith stared at him. "And what if you don't catch such a fish?"

"Then I'll treat you like a princess."

"Oh, I'll agree to that." She laughed. "I wouldn't mind being treated like a princess. You start anytime you're ready."

"Done."

Leaping to his feet, Alex waded out into the water. For some time he had been watching a big log almost like the one where he and Reb had caught the catfish. He had even seen a catfish roll over here, so he knew they were there. *Now I must do some serious noodling*, he thought.

He was sure Lilith could not imagine what he was doing. When he leaned over and put his hands under the log, she yelled at him. "You'll never catch fish like that! You lose!"

Alex said nothing but kept feeling under the log. Once he touched a fish, but it moved away beyond his reach. Finally, though, he felt what surely was a huge catfish. *Must weigh ten pounds!* he thought.

Gently he rubbed the fish's stomach and felt him grow very still. Stealthily he moved his hand up and reached under its chin. He was careful about touching the huge spikes, because he knew that it would be bad if he was poisoned by one of them. He waited until his thumb was inside the catfish's mouth. Then he clamped down exactly as he had done before. At once the fish closed its jaws, and he felt the rough edge of tiny teeth.

He dragged the fish out from under the log, but this time did not attempt to throw it to shore. It was too large for that. He simply backed away, pulling his huge catch after him, while the catfish thrashed the water white.

When Alex reached knee-deep water, he looked over his shoulder and grinned at Lilith. "How about this? Think it'll feed us all?" And now, with a quick throw, he sailed the fish through the air. It struck the bushes and began flopping about. He waded onto shore and waited until he could safely kill the fish. Then, holding it up, he turned to Lilith. "I win the wager, I believe."

She appeared absolutely shocked and astounded. "Yes, you do," she gasped.

"You can start paying off right now. I'm the prince, remember, and I demand to be treated as such." He dropped the fish and watched Lilith to see what she would do. He knew she was a strong-minded girl and pride was in her, too. He saw the hesitation in her eyes and knew that this would be hard for her. "Oh, it's all right, Lilith," he said. "It was just for fun. You don't have to pay any penalty."

"Yes, I do!"

She stepped forward and with a graceful motion curtsied before him. "My prince, I honor you. You are the best fisherman I have ever seen."

Alex took her hand and lifted her up. "It's all right. You don't have to go through with this," he said gently.

"I always do exactly what I promise. I may be poor, but I can keep my word."

He should have known. Lilith was a girl of strict honor who kept her word. And she would have extracted the penalty from him if *he* had lost.

Alex was tremendously impressed. "Well, let's take it home," he said. "This fish will be very good." He leaned over to pick it up.

But Lilith beat him to it. "Oh no, Prince. I'll carry the fish. And you go before me—it would not be fitting that I should walk with you."

"Oh, come now, Lilith! Don't be ridiculous."

"That's the way it is. The prince goes first, and his followers come after. Let us go home."

They made their way back to the big house with Lilith walking a few paces behind him and carrying the catfish. He kept urging her to forget about the silly wager, but he could see that her mind was made up. When they reached the house, he said, "You have kept your bargain. Now give me the fish. I'll clean it."

"Oh no, sire. I am your handmaid." She bowed low. "Enter the house, Your Majesty. *I* will clean the fish."

"Oh, I wish you wouldn't act like this!" Alex growled. He went around to the bunkhouse and washed up. By the time he got back to the big house, Lilith was already cooking the fish. As he entered, he saw Joss and Sarah smiling and knew that he was in for it. "We made this silly wager . . ." he said but could not finish.

Lilith came across the room, pulled out a chair and said, "Here is your throne, O royal prince. Sit down and your subjects will feed you."

His face hot, Alex mumbled, "This is nonsense!"

"Oh no, sire. It is only right. You are royalty, and I am only a poor peasant girl."

Sarah giggled. Lilith's father was grinning.

The meal was fine. The fish was tender and delicious, but Alex did not enjoy it. Lilith refused to sit down and eat. She stood behind him and constantly filled his cup and saw to it that he had the best of the fish and vegetables. She urged him on, calling him "sire" and "Your Majesty" and "Prince Lex."

Finally Alex had enough. He left his chair, picked her up bodily, and set her on the high, narrow mantel. She barely had room to cling to it.

"Put me down!"

"Only if you do what I tell you."

"And what's that?" she challenged.

"Stop acting as you have been doing. Just treat me like Lex."

To his surprise, she smiled and said sweetly, "All right, Lex. Help me down." Perhaps she could tell that he was really embarrassed. When he had lifted her down, as if she were a feather, she said, "My, you're very strong."

"All right. Now let's have some dessert."

"It's apple pie," Sarah said. "Now that we've got all that foolishness out of the way, maybe you'll enjoy it better."

Afterward Sarah found a chance to speak with Alex alone. "That was dangerous. You shouldn't have told her you were the prince."

"I *didn't* tell her I was the prince," he said. "It was a game. I just told her to treat me like one if I won the fish wager. Just for part of the day."

"Well, I don't think she thought anything about it. Still, it was dangerous."

"She's a nice girl, isn't she, Sarah?"

"As well as one of the prettiest girls I've ever seen." She looked into the prince's face. "I don't think she's like the girls that you knew at the palace. I hope you don't treat her like a . . . a common woman."

Alex was truly shocked. "How could you ever think such a thing! Of course I won't. She's a fine girl, a special girl—even though she *is* a peasant."

"Back in OldWorld there were cases where princes married girls who were not of the royal blood."

"Is that right? It never happens in this place." He thought about that for a moment, though. "Well, she's a fine person, and I'll be sad when we have to say good-bye."

12

The Secret Weapon

The Zorian battle chief drew himself up proudly and looked around at his officers. They made a ring around him, all large men clad in armor and wearing the symbol of the Dark Lord on their tunics, and they watched him closely. Chief Thomor was the largest of them all. As he gazed around, looking for some weakness in his leaders, he found none. He said in a loud, hoarse voice, "Today is the day!"

A loud cheer went up from the officers, and they raised their swords in a symbol of victory.

"We will end this war today!"

Another cheer, and then Thomor asked his lieutenant, a short bulky soldier with murky brown eyes, "Is all ready?"

"Yes, Thomor. All is ready."

"And is the beast ready?"

"Ready," the lieutenant said confidently.

Thomor felt called upon to make a speech. "We have waited long for this day. Our enemies have kept us out, but today we will storm the pass, and we will possess the land. Some of us will die, but it is a good thing to die for one's country."

The speech went on for some time until finally Thomor said, "Now, let us inspire the troops by our presence."

As they left the guardroom, the masses of soldiers lined up outside, rank on rank, uttered a cheer.

"As you see, the troops are ready, Thomor," the lieutenant said.

"Good. Officers, take your places. It is the hour of the beast!"

Alcindor was a man of great physical courage, but today he felt apprehensive. He sensed that the Zorian soldiers massed behind the mountain passes were about to move, though he had seen nothing that would tell him this.

His first officer, a tall man named Glein, must have seen something in his commander's eyes. "What is it, Alcindor?" Glein asked. "You seem nervous."

"Something's happening, and I don't know what it is."

"There's nothing that we know of. No further report has come from the front." But at the very moment Glein spoke, two soldiers came in. A small man was between them.

"Ah, it's our good agent Danan. Danan, what news?"

Danan had deep-sunk brown eyes and scraggly brown hair and was clothed in the garb of a peasant. No one would ever notice him in a crowd, but Alcindor knew him to be an excellent scout. The man could move silently and almost invisibly.

The agent stopped and touched his forehead in a salute. "There is news, Alcindor," he said. "The Zorians are moving their men to the pass by the twin oaks. They will make their attack there, I believe."

"Did you see anything of a secret weapon?"

"No," admitted Danan. "I could not get that close—their scouts are out in great numbers. But the Zorian troops are moving that way."

"Good work, Danan," Alcindor said warmly. He

turned to Glein. "We'll move our best archers to the twin oaks."

"What about the other passes?" Glein asked. "Should we leave them unguarded?"

"Leave a few men at each to give the alarm and hold long enough to shift our army if necessary. But we will go on Danan's word. He has never failed us."

Quickly the message went out, and within a short time Alcindor himself was at the pass of the twin oaks. These were two enormous trees that marked the narrow gap used as a passageway through the mountains. It had been impossible for the Zorians to storm this in the past, for here the Madrian archers could position themselves to shoot without exposing themselves.

Quickly Alcindor and Glein arranged their men in ranks. Alcindor gave careful instructions. "Expect them to force their way through. The men in our front line will shoot their arrows, then fall back. The second line will have arrows on strings and let go another volley, then fall back. We will have three lines so that there will always be a shower of arrows upon the enemy."

"It's a good plan," Danan said. He clawed his whiskers thoughtfully. "Something may be different about their attack this time. I've heard about some kind of secret weapon or troops, some surprise that the Zorians are going to spring on us . . ."

"We'll meet them, whatever it is." Then Alcindor lifted his voice, crying out, "Men, we must hold this line! We *will* hold!"

A cheer went up, and the soldiers began to shout loudly, "For the name of the king!"

"I would that King Alquin were here," Danan said.

"So do I, but he is not."

The two men stood waiting silently, and then

Alcindor saw one of the advance scouts scrambling back from over the pass. The man's eyes were wide, and he shouted, "They're coming!"

"How many?" Alcindor demanded, when the scout reached him, panting.

"I don't know. I didn't stop. They have a fearful *beast* at the head of them. I never saw anything like it."

Alcindor saw men in the nearby ranks waver. They were superstitious, he knew, and he cried, "Do not be afraid! Hold your line!" He himself advanced, planted his feet, and kept his eyes fixed on the gap.

Soon he could hear the sound of marching feet. He also heard voices raised in a battle song, coming loud and clear. Carefully he placed his best arrow on the string and stood waiting.

The noise grew louder. Then he saw something move, but he could not tell what it was for a moment. Then he did see—and, stalwart as he was, his heart skipped a beat.

A cry went up from the enemy then. "The beast has come, Madrians! The beast is here!"

What Alcindor saw was terrifying indeed. He had never seen an animal larger than a bull, but this creature was much larger than that. It was surely larger than even the OldWorld elephants he'd heard about.

The creature was gray with reddish eyes. Its back rose like a tower and was covered with huge armored plates. Its legs were thick as trees and had great claws that dug into the ground as it came. They were claws big enough to grasp a man. It had a long snout and a mouth full of sharp teeth.

So this was the secret weapon that the Dark Lord has fashioned for the Zorians. It was a mutant, no doubt, from the time the earth had been torn by atomic warfare.

"Stand fast! Make your arrows count!" Alcindor cried. "Aim for the riders if you can!"

A platform had been harnessed to the monster's back on which at least six men wearing armor were poised. They were archers and already had lifted their bows. Now they loosed a flight of arrows, and Alcindor saw three of his men fall.

"Shoot!" he cried, and a flight of Madrian arrows filled the air. They were all concentrated either on the beast or on its riders—and none of them took effect. The animal's heavy plates and the men's body armor turned every arrow harmlessly aside.

Again the enemy riders loosed their shafts with deadly aim.

Alcindor knew at once that the situation was desperate. He shouted, "Keep up your fire! The troops will come in behind the creature if we let it advance."

The mammoth beast kept on coming through the narrow pass. Arrows struck it by the hundreds, but all were turned aside.

And then Alcindor glimpsed the Zorian infantry advancing behind the beast. He ran forward as if daring the enemy to shoot. He put an arrow to his string and, breathing a plea to Goél for help, loosed it. "Shoot!" he ordered the men behind him. "Shoot!"

Another line of Madrian archers shot and fell back, and a new line took their place. It was a steep pass, which was part of its advantage to the Madrians. The beast was having to climb upward as it came.

The battle raged. A few brave men advanced to the very feet of the beast. It seized one of them with its trunk.

At last, at close range and with an enormous flight of arrows, the men on the platform were brought down. Strangely, the beast now seemed uncertain. Perhaps it had been trained to obey the voice of one on its back, and now there was no voice to obey. The Zorians' secret weapon hesitated, then slowly turned and lumbered back down the narrow pass.

"We won!" Glein said. "We beat them!"

"No, they will be back, and we did not hurt the beast at all," Alcindor said grimly. "They'll find some way to fight their way through."

"What can we do?"

"I must report to the king. You're in command, Glein, until I return."

Alcindor made a hard ride back to the city. Having thundered over the bridge and thrown himself off his steed, he raced up to the throne room. There he found King Alquin awaiting his report, and Alcindor poured it out without pausing. "And so we managed to hold, though we lost many good archers."

"But the beast will be back," the king said wearily.

"I fear so. And then, unless a miracle happens, all is lost."

The king summoned Count Ferrod and Ferrod's close friend Asimov, the captain of the armies, who also had come in from the field. Asimov had not been in the battle, but he listened as Alcindor described it.

"We *must* find a way to fight this terrible creature," the king said.

"There is no way, if what Alcindor says is true," Ferrod said quickly. "A beast that cannot be killed with arrows is beyond us."

"I fear Count Ferrod is right," the captain put in. "We can only surrender and make terms."

"Never!" the king cried.

The argument became heated, but at the end King Alquin bowed his head in thought while everyone waited for his decision. Then the king looked up and said, "You are dismissed from your office, Asimov. The new captain will be Alcindor."

Anger flashed in the captain's eyes, and he began to protest. But the king said, "That is all. Alcindor, our fate lies in your hands."

When Chief Thomor reported to Rondel what had happened in the battle, Rondel grunted. "So we did not win the victory. I am displeased."

Thomor shrugged. "It was just the first attempt. We destroyed at least fifty of them, and we lost only six men ourselves. They cannot keep losing troops like that."

"But the victory must be won quicker than this. Find some way to protect the men riding the beast. And I want the next attack made as soon as possible."

"There will be no stopping the beast, Rondel. And once we break through the pass and the beast is loosed among the Madrians, my men will pour through like a flood."

"Make it soon," Rondel said. "The Dark Lord is impatient."

13
The True Prince

I like this place," Alex said. "I have never known a place where I could come and feel such peace."

Lilith leaned back against a huge tree that arched over the river and closed her eyes. It was early afternoon, and the hot sun burned on the land. But it was cool here in the shadow of the tree, and the gurgling of the stream was a pleasant and delightful sound.

"I love it here, too," she said quietly.

Lilith had never been drawn to anyone as she had been to this tall, auburn-haired youth who had come into her life. In fact, the two had grown very close during the days that he had been at the farm. Now she looked up at him and laughed. "There's a bug in your hair," she said. She leaned close and picked the bug out.

"Did you know you have freckles?" he asked, looking at her nose.

"I do know. When I was a little girl, I was ashamed of them. One time I made a flour paste and put it over my face. My father and mother laughed at me. Father said freckles are cute, but I hated them."

Alex put a finger on the bridge of her nose. "You have a cute nose," he said. "But, yes, there are a few freckles." Then he said thoughtfully, "Lilith, these days here at your home have been very good for me."

"They've been good for me too," she said. "What are you going to do with your life when you leave here, Lex?" she asked suddenly. "You weren't made to be a farmhand. You were made for better things. I've always known that."

"I may have been made for better things, but I've wasted my life."

And then Lilith said, as she had once before, "But a person can change."

He was about to answer, but he had no opportunity. In the distance, a rider was charging down the lane that led to the farmhouse.

"Somebody's in a hurry," Alexander said. "Shall we go see who it is?"

Lilith peered at the horseman. "It's—it's Alcindor."

"We'd better go quickly, then."

They ran across the field and arrived at the house just as Alcindor reached it from the road. His horse was streaked with foam and panting.

Alcindor came down from the horse in one swift movement. "Prince Alexander," he said, "I have bad news."

Lilith's father was at the door, gaping. "P–Prince Alexander?" he stuttered.

Alex glanced at Lilith, who appeared stunned. She could only stare at him. He said quietly, "Yes, Lilith. I am the prince."

"The true prince?" she whispered.

"The true prince! Of course he's the true prince!" Alcindor cried. "And there's no time for idle talk. Everything has gone bad, my Prince."

"What's happened, Alcindor?"

"For some time we've been hearing that the Zorians have a secret weapon. Now they have launched it at us, and we've suffered a terrible defeat. We lost many good men, and we are going to lose more."

Alcindor gave a brief report of the Zorians' "weapon"

—a savage beast. He told them how the battle had gone. And then he said glumly, "I fear all is lost, Prince Alexander. The next attack the beast makes, he will break through our lines. Once he is through the pass, our men will flee. They cannot stand against him."

Everyone's eyes were on Alex, who stood absolutely still. His life seemed to flash before his eyes. He bitterly regretted the wasted years and wished with all his heart that he had been different. Then he turned to Lilith. "You told me," he said, "that a person can change."

"Yes," she said quietly, still apparently trying to put together in her mind what she had heard of the prince, who lived for nothing but pleasure, and the young man she knew as Lex. "He can."

Prince Alexander of Madria drew himself up to his full height, and his eyes held those of Alcindor. "We will raise an army from among the people. We will put a mighty host at the pass."

"They will fear the beast. It is a frightening creature, sire."

"I will call every man in this kingdom to arms to save our country. Quick, Joss, we must have horses, and then I want to talk to all the men in the village."

Alcindor seemed shocked. But that was understandable, Alexander thought. Alcindor had seldom seen him do anything but enjoy himself.

Lilith said, "I will go to the village with you."

In the village, Alexander stood in the center of the marketplace, raised his sword, and shouted, "I am the prince of Madria! Our country is in danger. Who will follow me to fight against this peril that would destroy our homes and our families?"

Alcindor listened to him, astonished. Where had this new quality in the young man come from? It was the quality of leadership, and it made the men of the village pay attention.

He said quietly to Joss and Lilith, "The prince has changed. He never cared anything about the kingdom before. But whatever it is that makes a leader, I see that he has it. His father had it like no one else I ever knew, and now I see that quality in the son."

They rode from village to village, stopping only briefly at each one. But in every place men listened to the prince, then joined him, some armed with bows, some with swords, some with pitchforks. The small volunteer army gathered strength as it headed toward the palace.

"I must go to my father," Prince Alexander told Alcindor. "Whatever happens with the beast, I must make my peace with my parents."

"I think that is well, and your father's heart will be gladdened," Alcindor said.

The volunteers moved along with the prince in the forefront, and at one point he looked back and saw Lilith. She now wore a sword at her side! Alexander went to her at once. "Lilith," he said, "this is not for you. Go home. Be safe."

She turned her green eyes upon him. "I will go with you, Prince Alexander."

Alex reached out his hand, and she took it. "Very well. So it shall be."

As soon as Sarah received the word from Alcindor, she gathered the other Sleepers. They caught up with the prince's army, if it could be called that, as it approached the palace.

"What's going on?" Josh cried, riding up to Alcindor.

"The prince has had a change of heart. This is the army he has raised."

"I know," Josh said with wonder. "But will it be enough?"

"I do not think so," Alcindor said quietly. "But we shall see."

The army that arrived at the palace would be called the Army of Peasants in future histories. Some would call it the Army of Prince Alexander. But in any case, when they neared the palace, Count Ferrod met them.

Ferrod stood before the gate, saying, "Who *is* this mob? Begone! You have no business at the palace!"

Then Prince Alexander stepped out of his saddle, wearing his peasant's clothing.

At first, Count Ferrod appeared shocked. But when he saw it was indeed the prince, he attempted to smile, saying, "Well, well, we have been searching everywhere for you."

"I'm sure you have, Count Ferrod," Alex said in an icy tone. "And I well know what you would have done with me had your men found me alone."

Ferrod tried to speak. After that, he swallowed hard, and then he fell to his knees. "Pardon, Prince Alex. I was misled . . ."

"I will deal with you later, but now I must go to my father."

Alex started again toward the palace, then suddenly paused and turned back. Quickly he lifted Lilith off her horse. "Come with me. You must meet my parents." He took her by the hand.

Lilith gave him a frightened look, but his hand held

hers tightly, and he pulled her along. When they came to the double doors, Alex glared at both guards. "Stand aside! I am the prince of Madria!"

Quickly the two exchanged glances and stepped aside.

As Alex and Lilith entered the throne room, his mother uttered a glad cry and threw herself into Alex's arms. She clung to him fiercely.

Then the prince went to the frail man who sat beside the window. His father looked ill, but there was a glad light in his eyes as Alex knelt beside him.

"Forgive me, my father, for I have been remiss. I have led the wrong life and not followed your example."

"My son!" King Alquin put his hands on the prince's hair. "You've come back to us."

Alex and his father stood to their feet, and the two embraced. Then the prince said, "I have indeed come back, and I am going to fight against Zor and their beast. I do not know whether we shall win or not, but we shall give our lives if need be to save our country."

Then he saw the queen's eyes go to Lilith.

Alex went at once to Lilith's side. "I want you to meet one who has helped me find myself. Lilith, my father and my mother—King Alquin and Queen Lenore."

Lilith would never have had lessons in court etiquette, but somehow she knew instinctively what to do. She curtsied with a graceful motion to the floor and bowed her head. "I am honored, Your Majesties," she murmured.

Queen Lenore went to her at once and raised her up. "How beautiful you are, child!" she whispered. "And you have been a help to our son?"

"Yes, she has," the prince said. "And I hope you will get to know one another better."

"I am sure we will," King Alquin said, coming himself to greet Lilith and take her hand.

At that moment Dethenor burst into the throne room, and behind him was Alcindor.

"My prince," Dethenor said, "you have returned!"

"Yes. I am come back. Now, what is to be done about the terrible beast of Zor?"

Dethenor looked at Alcindor, who said, "Unless it can be killed, we are lost."

For some reason, everyone looked at the prince. It was still a new thing to him, this somehow expecting him to assume the mantle of authority. He stood tall and strong with his clear eyes fastened on them and said, "Then the beast must be killed!"

14

Reb's Plan

Along with Dethenor and Alcindor, the prince was meeting with the Council to decide on what steps to take. At the same time, the Sleepers had drawn themselves apart into a room alone.

Jake said, "What I wouldn't give to have one Sherman tank here. That would take care of that beast!"

"Why don't you wish for an atom bomb?" Dave groaned. "We don't have either one, and we won't have."

Many plans of action had been brought up and then cast aside as useless. Josh thought everyone looked discouraged.

Wash had been sitting quietly, just listening to the talk. He said, "We can't give up. Goél's never failed us. He's always shown us what to do. Always. And not too late, either."

"You're right, of course. He has," Josh said, thankful for Wash's cheerful spirit. Wash was always one of the most optimistic of the Sleepers. "What we need Goél to show us right now is some plan to get rid of the beast. And we won't have any hand grenades or bombs to do it with."

The conversation went on for some time, but nothing came of it. Everyone was sure that on the next day there would be some sort of attack by the Zorian beast, but so far there seemed to be nothing they could do about it.

The Sleepers were all exhausted after their long ride. Finally, everybody just went to bed.

* * *

Reb lay awake on his blanket for a long time. His mind ranged from one possible solution to another, but none of them seemed to be worth considering. Finally he drifted off to sleep. For a while he even dreamed—about alligators. It was a vivid dream, too. He could see and hear and smell the things that took place.

Then Reb woke up with a start and was amazed to find an idea in his mind. He let out his shrill Rebel yell, jumped up, and did a little dance.

Josh came to his feet, staring around wildly. Then he saw Reb. "What's wrong with you, Reb? Have you lost your mind?"

"Lost my mind! No, I haven't lost my mind!" He pounded Josh on the chest, so hard that Josh stepped back. Then he continued his little dance.

The others came rushing from their various sleeping places.

Sarah grabbed his arms. "Reb, you're acting like a maniac. What's wrong with you?"

"Nothing's wrong with me. Now I know how to kill that old beast."

"What are you talking about?" Jake sounded cross at getting waked up.

Reb finally calmed somewhat, though he was still so excited he could hardly stand still. "I said I know how to kill the Zorians' beast," he repeated.

"How?" Josh asked. "Tell us if you think you know something."

"I got the idea from a dream."

"He had a dream," Dave groaned. "That's all we need, a dreamer."

But Josh said, "Wait. What's your idea, Reb?"

"Well, I dreamed about the time I was hunting alligators down in Louisiana with my Cousin Boudreaux. He was a Cajun, and I'll tell you what—he really knew something about alligators."

"Alligators! What's alligators got to do with the Zorians' beast?" Jake grumbled.

"Let him tell it," Wash broke in. "What about alligators?"

"Well, my cousin hunted them with spears. They had such a tough hide on the back that we couldn't pierce them on top. What he would do is he would roll them over and stab 'em on the underside. Same way with armadillos back in Texas," he said. "They're tough on the top, but underneath they're soft. Same way maybe with the Zorians' beast."

"You could be right," Josh said, rubbing his chin. "But there's one problem with it."

"What's that?"

"Well, as far as we know, this critter runs on four legs, and it's got big legs and claws. How would we ever get to his underside?"

"That's where the beauty of my idea comes in." Reb grinned.

"The beauty of it?" Abbey said. "What's beautiful about a beast?"

"It'll be beautiful to get him. What I figure is," Reb said, "if we can get him to rear up, we can nail him with spears on that soft underbelly."

"But how are we going to get him to rear up?"

Reb looked at Wash, who had asked the question. "I'll tell you how. What we'll do is this: I'll drop a noose over his head and pull him up, and while I'm holding him up, you guys rush in and spear him."

Everyone groaned, and Josh shook his head in

despair. "Reb, didn't you listen to what Alcindor said? This is a *monstrous* thing! Nobody's going to drop a rope around its neck and pull it up. In the first place, it'd break the rope. In the second place, nobody's strong enough."

"I know that," Reb said. "Do you think I don't know that? What we do is make a cable of some kind. A *really* thick rope. Maybe out of metal. Anyway, we put a noose in it. We run through the noose through a pulley—"

"I got it!" Jake said. "It's a work of art!"

"What's a work of art?" Josh demanded.

"Don't you see?" Jake asked. "We attach that cable to a bunch of horses. Then, when Reb drops that noose around the critter's neck, we start those horses pulling. And *they'll* haul him up, I'll bet you."

For a moment there was silence, and then Jake let out another yell. "It'll work. I tell you it'll work." He leaped at Reb, almost knocking him over, and then everyone gathered around the tall Southerner, beating him on the back and praising him.

"Well, that's one dream that came in handy," Reb said. "Do you reckon Goél gave me that idea?"

Josh said. "That could be exactly where the idea came from. We've got to tell the prince right away."

The Sleepers went at once to where the Council was meeting with Prince Alexander. King Alquin and Queen Lenore themselves were seated at the table, though the king looked pale and weak.

Josh had Reb explain his plan, and Jake broke in more than once with a refinement of the scheme. When the boys finished, the Council sat stunned.

"I've never heard of such tactics," Alcindor said.

"We've never heard of a beast like this, either," the

prince said grimly. He turned to Jake and Reb. "Could you two make such a device?"

"We sure could."

"There's only one problem left," Josh said. "We can set up the trap that will snare the beast, but how can we be sure he will come through that particular pass?"

The prince thought for a moment, as all eyes were upon him. And then he smiled. "I will send a challenge to the Zorians. I will tell them that the prince of Madria himself will be at the west pass. That is the narrowest pass through the mountains. There will be barely room for the beast to get through, and there is an overhang where we can arrange your device, Jake and Reb."

"I believe the scheme will work." The speaker that time was King Alquin. "Go, my son," the king said. "Uphold the honor of the royal family."

"I will, Father." The prince arose and said, "Alcindor, send a courier at once, challenging the Zorians. Tell them we will meet them at the west pass and that the prince of Madria himself will stand against the beast."

15

The Battle of the Beast

All night long and into the dawn hours, Reb and Jake directed the construction of the snare for the terrible beast of Zor. Jake seemed to be everywhere, shouting instructions, calling for material.

At one point, Alcindor, watching him, said to the prince, "I never saw such activity. That boy is exceptional."

The prince, however, was staring at the pulley that Jake and his helpers were installing on a timber that had been placed across the pass. "Do you think this scheme will really work?" he asked with a worried look in his eye.

"I truly don't know, but it's the only hope we have."

Then Alexander left him, to move among the soldiers and encourage them. And Alcindor thought that to be an admirable thing.

During his walking about, Prince Alexander came to where Lilith stood apart from a line of archers. He said, "Are you free? Walk with me, Lilith."

"All right, my prince."

He laughed. "Do you remember when I won our wager?"

"Yes, I do," she said quietly. "But I never thought I'd be walking with the true prince of Madria."

They walked up and down, cheering the troops. Finally they reached the end of the lines and started back. "I may not be able to say this later . . ." Alexander began.

* * *

Abbey stood off to one side with Dave, watching Lilith walking with the prince. "Isn't love wonderful?" she sighed.

Dave gave her a disgusted look. "We're about to get killed by a horrendous beast, and you think it's all a movie! You think all the world is *Gone with the Wind*, Abbey."

"I loved that film. How I would love to live in a house like that and come sweeping down that staircase . . ."

Josh and Sarah overheard what Abbey said, and Sarah smiled. "She'll never change. She's the world's greatest romantic."

"I guess she is."

For a time, they watched the men working at completing the snare. Then they walked over to the horses that had been brought in to haul the beast into the air. They had great fuzzy hooves and were strongly built and looked totally capable.

"They're beautiful horses," Sarah said.

"Yes, they are. I hope they can do their job."

Jake and Reb stood on the crest of the hill, talking. They studied the strong cable that they had constructed. There was no way to test it, nor was there time.

"Well, we're as ready as we can be with Goél's idea," Reb said. He picked up the rope and, although it was much thicker than a lariat, he formed a noose with a slipknot.

"Do you think you can rope with that thing, Reb?" Jake asked worriedly.

"I ain't never missed."

"Oh yes you have," Jake corrected him.

"Well, maybe a few times. But I couldn't miss anything as big as that monster. All I have to do is spread a big noose and drop it over his head. And, Jake, when you see that noose tighten up, you drive those horses like crazy."

"I wish we had elephants to pull up that critter."

"Well, we don't. And it'll be up to the prince and the others down below to get in and spear the varmint. I hope I was right about that tender underbelly."

"I hope so, too," Jake said. "Well, here's another fine mess we've gotten ourselves into."

At the bottom of the hill, Alcindor was giving final instructions. "I want all of you archers to pepper the men on that platform on the beast's back. Don't give them a chance to get off a shot. Keep them thrown off balance." Then he turned to Alexander. "Arrows will not do it, my prince. It will have to be these." He picked up a spear made out of fine ash. It was eight feet long and was barbed with a keen tip. "I hope these will do it, and we won't know until we have tried."

The prince picked up one of the spears and balanced it in his hand. "It seems a good weapon," he said.

Alcindor bit his lip. "My prince, I have to say something to you."

"Say on, Alcindor. What is it?"

"I beg you. Do not go in with the spearmen. If I am lost, or if any other man is lost, it is only one life. But you are the heir to the throne. If you are lost, everyone will lose heart."

But Prince Alex shook his head. "One cannot lead from behind. A king must be in the forefront of the battle. You know that, Alcindor. You saw my father do it."

They had no time for further talk. A cry sounded from the sentry then, faint but clear enough for them to hear him.

"The beast—the beast is coming!"

"Everyone in position!" Prince Alex cried. He looked upward and asked, "Reb, are you ready?"

"Ready. Jake, get down there, and when you see that noose drop, drive those horses!"

Everyone got into place. Jake stood ready beside the men who were holding the ten horses. They had rigged a mighty hitch that would throw the weight of all the horses into action at once. The cable ran upward, hidden by the rise of the pass, and then went through a pulley.

The plan was for Reb not to go out yet on the timber that spanned the gap, for fear he would be seen. He would have to wait until the last minute to do that.

Then the sound of marching feet and the shouts of soldiers came toward the pass, growing stronger every minute. The prince watched and waited.

"Here they come!" He lifted his voice, shouting, "Every man stand fast for king, for country, and for family!"

A yell went up from the Madrian troops, and the prince's eyes met those of Alcindor. "Our men are firm. They will stand and do all they can."

"I think you're right, my prince."

Abruptly Alexander said, "Alcindor, quickly! I gathered a large number of volunteers. I want to send half of them around the ends of our lines."

"But why would you do this?"

"They will do more good there. If we kill the beast here at the pass and then our volunteers come up behind the Zorian troops, we will have them in a pincer. We can crush Zor once and for all."

"That's good strategy!" Alcindor exclaimed. "I will see to it at once."

So half the army of Madria faded away to the flanks. They would circle around and make their way through the forest behind the Zorian lines. Zor would be taken by surprise. The Madrian army had never attacked before, and there was no reason to think they would now.

The beast of Zor came into view then, snorting and uttering hoarse cries. His huge claws dug into the path as he climbed upward. On his back stood the archers, poised and ready. It was a frightening sight.

Josh and Sarah watched the beast come toward them. "We've never fought anything like that before," he murmured. "Never."

"But we will," she said and suddenly took his hand. "We've been through so much together, it can't end here. Now Goél will show what he can do."

Josh kept his eye on the beam that spanned the gap overhead. The beast's head would pass no more than ten feet below it. It had occurred to him more than once that if Reb were seen, the soldiers might get the beast to rear up and attack him.

The monster came on, roaring, roaring, and behind it marched the Zorian soldiers, bearing spears and swords.

Close to the timber bridge, Reb remained hidden with the noose spread in his hand. His breath was coming short as he watched the Beast climb steadily upward through the pass. A few more steps now, and he would be underneath the beam.

He waited until the last moment, then walked swiftly but carefully out to the middle of the beam. The beast must have sensed the movement above, for it stopped and looked up. At that moment, Reb dropped the noose over the creature's head and screamed, "Pull, Jake! Pull for all you're worth!"

Jake saw the noose settle around the beast's neck, and he cried, "Pull, you horses!" The horse handlers struck the draft horses lightly, and the mighty animals obediently threw themselves against their collars.

Jake was watching the noose tighten around the beast's neck. Surely everyone was watching. Would the timber hold? Would the pulley do its job?

A terrible struggle ensued then, the horses pulling, their masters encouraging them, the rope stretching as tight as a rope could be stretched. The beast was powerful. It tried to bite the cable under its chin but could not get at it.

But the archers had seen Reb, and one of them cried, "Get him! Get him!"

Arrows flew through the air, but Reb flattened himself on the beam so that they went harmlessly by. "Pull, Jake—pull! We got him!" he yelled.

The titanic struggle went on, for the beast was monstrously strong. But the horses were strong, too, and suddenly the prince yelled, "Look at the beast's front feet! They're off the ground!"

A cheer went up. The horses, with their great combined strength, had indeed managed to get the creature's front claws free from the ground. Their masters shouted, and the hooves of the mighty horses clawed at the dust as they strained against their collars.

* * *

Up—up—up went the beast, until the prince saw its yellow underside. "Forward, spearmen!" he cried and raced forward himself with Alcindor at his side.

The spearmen and the Seven Sleepers too, all themselves bearing spears, dashed toward the exposed belly of the beast. Its huge claws clawed the air, its hind claws dug into the earth, and the creature was uttering mighty bellows of pain and anger. There was now no chance for the archers on the beast's back to use their bows and arrows, for they were being tilted backward. One man actually fell from the platform to the ground.

Alcindor drew back his spear and drove it with all of his might. Others hurled their spears. But the underside of the beast was plated, too. The plating was not as thick as that on the back and sides, but it was hard and slippery.

And then the hind claws of the beast caught the prince and threw him headlong. Alexander struggled to his feet and cried, "Try again!"

Zorian soldiers, archers with drawn bows, now were edging around the beast in order to attack. The Madrian archers moved closer and fought them off.

Surely none of them would ever forget the battle that took place that day. The huge beast kept swinging about on its hind legs and clawing at the cable.

But now the struggle swayed against the Madrians. The horses could not hold the heavy beast. It seemed to be gaining its footing again. And more Zorian infantry was pouring in from behind.

In desperation the prince looked up at the beast's underside. "There!" he cried. "Just inside the front legs there is no armor! Lift me up. Quick!"

At once Alcindor and Dave seized the prince by the legs and boosted him upward. Alex drew back his spear and thrust it forward with all his strength.

The beast let out a mighty scream. It thrashed around. It gave a great shudder, making one last swing with its claws that knocked down all three of them.

But the terrible beast was no more.

Alcindor helped the prince to his feet, and Alexander yelled in triumph, "The beast is dead! Madria, attack!"

The prince and all who had fought against the beast were weary, but they pressed forward. The archers did their work, and then the volunteers the prince had gathered struck the Zorians from behind.

A cry of terror went up from the enemy troops, and the Zorians began to flee.

But one Zorian did not flee. Rondel stood tall, trying to rally the troops. He found himself suddenly face to face with the prince of Madria.

"Ah, Alexander," he said. And he raised his sword.

The prince engaged him. They fought viciously, and then Alexander lost his balance on a slippery spot and fell.

Instantly Rondel was on him with his blade. "I win, and you lose!"

But the sword never descended. An arrow made a whizzing sound, and Rondel slumped to the ground, dropping his weapon.

The prince got to his feet and turned to see Lilith lowering her bow. He went to her, saying, "Your skills amaze me. It's going to take a lifetime to learn how to deal with you."

Lilith was pale, but she managed a smile. "Well, I have a lifetime, my prince!"

16

Last Words

The Sleepers had never enjoyed anything more than the days that followed the destruction of the beast and the defeat of Zor. It had been a complete victory, and now it was the Zorians who were under the military government of the Madrians. There had been celebrating and feasts, and the only dark hour was when the king banished Count Ferrod.

King Alquin stripped the count of his honors, saying, "You deserve death, but you are my kinsman. Instead, you are banished from my kingdom forever."

Aside from that, all was enjoyable.

The time came, however, when Josh knew that it was time to leave. They had one final time of good-byes with the friends that they had made in Madria and made promises to come back if they could.

Then the Sleepers rode back toward the sea, where they planned to resume their vacation.

As they rode along, Reb suddenly said to Wash, "I wish I could have had that critter mounted."

"What critter?" Wash asked. "The *beast?*"

"The beast. Of course he'd be too big to keep, I guess. And he would take a lot of stuffing."

Wash laughed aloud. "You think of the craziest things. Who would want to stuff that thing?"

"Well, they had Stonewall Jackson's horse stuffed. Little Sorrel. And Roy Rogers had Trigger stuffed. He's in a museum. I saw him once."

"I think Trigger and Little Sorrel are a little bit different from the beast of Zor. I never want to see that thing again—alive or dead."

Abbey was riding on the other side of Reb. She sniffed. "A fine romance between a prince and a peasant girl, and all you two can talk about is stuffing beasts and horses!"

But Reb just smiled. "All in all, it was quite a party."

Wash reached over and slapped him on the shoulder. "I'll say this. You did good, Reb. Your dream idea was what pulled it off."

"You didn't do bad with those horses, either. But the ideas—we know where they really came from. As usual, Goél gave us the right ideas just when we needed them."

"It could have turned out so different," Jake went on. "The noose could have broken, or you could have missed."

"Wait a minute. I never miss!"

"Sure you do."

Josh and Sarah, riding in the lead, could hear Reb and Wash arguing. When they had pulled their horses slightly ahead, Josh said, "I've learned a lot from our adventures in NuWorld, Sarah. Mostly, I've learned I can always count on Goél. He hasn't made a mistake yet. And I learned something else from this last adventure."

"What's that, Josh?"

"I learned that I was just about as bad as Alex, wanting my own way."

"Yes, I guess you were," she said placidly.

"You don't have to agree with me so quick!"

Sarah laughed and whacked his arm. "You're *my* prince," she said. "But I'm glad you learned something.

We all did, Josh." And then a twinkle of fun came into her eyes. "Now you won't mind cooking dinner for me and serving me and bowing down. It'll be good for your humility."

Josh knew she was teasing. He laughed, and the two rode on, the other Sleepers following. And presently all disappeared under a canopy of trees as the sun beat down.

Get swept away in the many Gilbert Morris Adventures available from Moody Press:

"Too Smart" Jones

4025-8	Pool Party Thief
4026-6	Buried Jewels
4027-4	Disappearing Dogs
4028-2	Dangerous Woman
4029-0	Stranger in the Cave
4030-4	Cat's Secret
4031-2	Stolen Bicycle
4032-0	Wilderness Mystery
4033-9	Spooky Mansion
4034-7	Mysterious Artist

Come along for the adventures and mysteries Juliet "Too Smart" Jones always manages to find. She and her other homeschool friends solve these great adventures and learn biblical truths along the way. Ages 9-14

Seven Sleepers - The Lost Chronicles

3667-6	The Spell of the Crystal Chair
3668-4	The Savage Game of Lord Zarak
3669-2	The Strange Creatures of Dr. Korbo
3670-6	City of the Cyborgs
3671-4	The Temptations of Pleasure Island
3672-2	Victims of Nimbo
3672-0	The Terrible Beast of Zor

More exciting adventures from the Seven Sleepers. As these exciting young people attempt to faithfully follow Goél, they learn important moral and spiritual lessons. Come along with them as they encounter danger, intrigue, and mystery. Ages 10-14

MOODY
The Name You Can Trust
1-800-678-8812 www.MoodyPress.org

Dixie Morris Animal Adventures

3363-4 Dixie and Jumbo
3364-2 Dixie and Stripes
3365-0 Dixie and Dolly
3366-9 Dixie and Sandy
3367-7 Dixie and Ivan
3368-5 Dixie and Bandit
3369-3 Dixie and Champ
3370-7 Dixie and Perry
3371-5 Dixie and Blizzard
3382-3 Dixie and Flash

Follow the exciting adventures of this animal lover as she learns more of God and His character through her many adventures underneath the Big Top. Ages 9-14

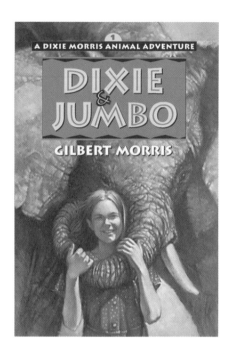

The Daystar Voyages

4102-X Secret of the Planet Makon
4106-8 Wizards of the Galaxy
4107-6 Escape From the Red Comet
4108-4 Dark Spell Over Morlandria
4109-2 Revenge of the Space Pirates
4110-6 Invasion of the Killer Locusts
4111-4 Dangers of the Rainbow Nebula
4112-2 The Frozen Space Pilot
4113-0 White Dragon of Sharnu
4114-9 Attack of the Denebian Starship

Join the crew of the Daystar as they traverse the wide expanse of space. Adventure and danger abound, but they learn time and again that God is truly the Master of the Universe. Ages 10-14

MOODY
The Name You Can Trust
1-800-678-8812 www.MoodyPress.org

Seven Sleepers Series

Go with Josh and his friends as they are sent by Goél, their spiritual leader, on dangerous and challenging voyages to conquer the forces of darkness in the new world. Ages 10-14

Bonnets and Bugles Series

Follow good friends Leah Carter and Jeff Majors as they experience danger, intrigue, compassion, and love in these civil war adventures. Ages 10-14

MOODY
The Name You Can Trust
1-800-678-8812 www.MoodyPress.org

Moody Press, a ministry of Moody Bible Institute,
is designed for education, evangelization, and edification.
If we may assist you in knowing more about Christ
and the Christian life, please write us without obligation:
Moody Press, c/o MLM, Chicago, Illinois 60610.